THE SPIRE

William Golding was born in Cornwall in 1911. He was educated at Marlborough Grammar School and at Brasenose College, Oxford, after which he worked as an actor, a lecturer, a small craft sailor, a musician, and finally a schoolmaster. A now rare volume, *Poems*, appeared in 1934. He joined the Royal Navy in 1940, and saw action against battleships, submarines and aircraft. He was present at the sinking of the Bismarck, and finished the war as a Lieutenant in command of a rocket ship. After the war he returned to Bishop Wordsworth's School in Salisbury and was there when his first novel, *Lord of the Flies*, was published in 1954. He gave up teaching in 1961, and went on to write twelve more novels, including *The Inheritors*, *Pincher Martin*, and *The Spire*.

Golding's play *The Brass Butterfly* was produced at the New Theatre, Oxford, in 1958, directed by Alistair Sim. *Lord of the Flies* was filmed by Peter Brook in 1963. Golding listed his hobbies as music, chess, sailing, archaeology and classical Greek (which he taught himself). Many of these subjects appear in his two collections of essays, *The Hot Gates*, and *A Moving Target*. He won the Booker Prize for his novel *Rites of Passage* in 1980, and was awarded the Nobel Prize for Literature in 1983. At this time he moved from the Wiltshire village where he had lived for half a century, to a fine house near Truro in Cornwall. He was knighted in 1988. He died at his home in the summer of 1993, leaving a draft of a novel, *The Double Tongue*, which was published posthumously.

by the same author

Fiction
LORD OF THE FLIES
THE INHERITORS
PINCHER MARTIN
FREE FALL
THE PYRAMID
THE SCORPION GOD
DARKNESS VISIBLE
THE PAPER MEN
RITES OF PASSAGE
CLOSE QUARTERS
FIRE DOWN BELOW
THE DOUBLE TONGUE
TO THE ENDS OF THE EARTH
(a revised text of *Rites of Passage, Close Quarters*
and *Fire Down Below* in one volume)

Essays
THE HOT GATES
A MOVING TARGET

Travel
AN EGYPTIAN JOURNAL

Play
THE BRASS BUTTERFLY

William Golding

The Spire

faber and faber

LONDON · BOSTON

First published in 1964
by Faber and Faber Limited
3 Queen Square London WC1N 3AU
First published in paperback in 1965

Printed and bound in Great Britain by
Mackays of Chatham PLC, Chatham, Kent

William Golding is hereby identified as author of this
work in accordance with Section 77 of the Copyright,
Designs and Patents Act 1988

A CIP record for this book
is available from the British Library

ISBN 0-571-19257-2

18 20 19 17

For JUDY

CHAPTER ONE

H e was laughing, chin up, and shaking his head. God the Father was exploding in his face with a glory of sunlight through painted glass, a glory that moved with his movements to consume and exalt Abraham and Isaac and then God again. The tears of laughter in his eyes made additional spokes and wheels and rainbows.

Chin up, hands holding the model spire before him, eyes half closed; joy —

'I've waited half my life for this day!'

Opposite him, the other side of the model of the cathedral on its trestle table stood the chancellor, his face dark with shadow, over ancient pallor.

'I don't know, my Lord Dean. I don't know.'

He peered across at the model of the spire, where Jocelin held it so firmly in both hands. His voice was bat-thin, and wandered vaguely into the large, high air of the chapter house.

'But if you consider that this small piece of wood — how long is it?'

'Eighteen inches, my Lord Chancellor.'

'Eighteen inches. Yes. Well. It represents, does it not, a construction of wood and stone and metal —'

'Four hundred feet high.'

The chancellor moved out into sunlight, hands up to

his chest, and peered round him. He looked up at the roof. Jocelin looked sideways at him, loving him.

'The foundations. I know. But God will provide.'

The chancellor had found what he was looking for, a memory.

'Ah yes.'

Then, in ancient busyness, he crept away over the pavement to the door and through it. He left a message, in the air behind him.

'Mattins. Of course.'

Jocelin stood still, and shot an arrow of love after him. My place, my house, my people. He will come out of the vestry at the tail of the procession and turn left as he has always done; then he will remember and turn right to the Lady Chapel! So Jocelin laughed again, chin lifted, in holy mirth. I know them all, know what they are doing and will do, know what they have done. All these years I have gone on, put the place on me like a coat.

He stopped laughing and wiped his eyes. He took the white spire and jammed it firmly in the square hole cut in the old model of the cathedral.

'There!'

The model was like a man lying on his back. The nave was his legs placed together, the transepts on either side were his arms outspread. The choir was his body; and the Lady Chapel where now the services would be held, was his head. And now also, springing, projecting, bursting, erupting from the heart of the building, there was its crown and majesty, the new spire. They don't know, he thought, they can't know until I tell them of my vision! And laughing again for joy, he went out of the chapter house to where the sun piled into the open square of the cloisters. And I must remember that the spire isn't

8

everything! I must do, as far as possible, exactly what I have always done.

So he went round the cloisters, lifting curtain after curtain, until he came to the side door into the West End of the cathedral. He lifted the latch carefully so as not to make a noise. He bowed his head as he passed through, and said as he always did interiorly, 'Lift up your heads, O ye Gates!' But even as he stepped inside, he knew that his caution was unnecessary, since there was a whole confusion of noise in the cathedral already. Mattins, diminished, its sounds so small they might be held in one hand, was nonetheless audible from the Lady Chapel at the other end of the cathedral, beyond the wood and canvas screen. There was a nearer sound that told — though the components were so mixed by echo as to be part of each other — that men were digging in earth and stone. They were talking, ordering, shouting sometimes, dragging wood across pavement, wheeling and dropping loads, then throwing them roughly into place, so that the total noise would have been formless as the noises of the market place, had not the echoing spaces made it chase round and round so that it caught up with itself and the shrill choir, and sang endlessly on one note. The noises were so new, that he hurried to the centre line of the cathedral in the shadow of the great west door, genuflected to the hidden High Altar; and then stood, looking.

He blinked for a moment. There had been sun before, but not like this. The most seeming solid thing in the nave, was not the barricade of wood and canvas that cut the cathedral in two, at the choir steps, was not the two arcades of the nave, nor the chantries and painted tomb slabs between them. The most solid thing was the light. It smashed through the rows of windows in the south

9

aisle, so that they exploded with colour, it slanted before him from right to left in an exact formation, to hit the bottom yard of the pillars on the north side of the nave. Everywhere, fine dust gave these rods and trunks of light the importance of a dimension. He blinked at them again, seeing, near at hand, how the individual grains of dust turned over each other, or bounced all together, like mayfly in a breath of wind. He saw how further away they drifted cloudily, coiled, or hung in a moment of pause, becoming, in the most distant rods and trunks, nothing but colour, honey-colour slashed across the body of the cathedral. Where the south transept lighted the crossways from a hundred and fifty foot of grisaille, the honey thickened in a pillar that lifted straight as Abel's from the men working with crows at the pavement.

He shook his head in rueful wonder at the solid sunlight. If it were not for that Abel's pillar, he thought, I would take the important level of light to be a true dimension, and so believe that my stone ship lay aground on her side; and he smiled a little, to think how the mind touches all things with law, yet deceives itself as easily as a child. Facing that barricade of wood and canvas at the other end of the nave, now that the candles have gone from the side altars, I could think this was some sort of pagan temple; and those two men posed so centrally in the sundust with their crows (and what a quarry noise and echo as they lever up the slab and let it fall back) the priests of some outlandish rite — Forgive me.

In this house for a hundred and fifty years, we have woven a rich fabric of constant praise. Things shall be as they were; only better, richer, the pattern of worship complete at last. I must go to pray.

And then he was aware that he would not go to pray yet,

even on this great day of joy. And he laughed aloud for pure joy, knowing why he would not go, knowing as of old, the daily pattern; knowing who was hunting, who preaching, who deputising for whom, knowing the security of the stone ship, the security of her crew.

As if the knowing was cue for entry in an interlude he heard a latch lift in the north-west corner and a door creak open. I shall see, as I see daily, my daughter in God..

Sure enough, as if his memory of her had called her in, she came quickly through the door, so that he stood, waiting with his blessing for her as always. But Pangall's wife turned to her left, lifted a hand against the dust. He had only time to glimpse the long, sweet face, before she had gone up the north aisle instead of coming straight across; so that he had to think his blessing after her. He watched her with love and a little disappointment as she passed the unlighted altars of the north aisle, saw her pull back her hood so that the white wimple showed, got a glimpse of green dress as the grey cloak swung back. She is entirely woman, he thought, loving her; and this foolish, this childish curiosity shows it. But that is a matter for Pangall or Father Anselm. And as if she recognised her own folly he saw how she circled the pit quickly, one hand up against the dust, crossed the nave and clashed the door of the Kingdom behind her. He nodded soberly.

'I suppose, after all, it must make some difference to us.'

After the clash of the door there was near-silence; then in the silence, a new little noise, tap, tap, tap. He turned to his left, and there the dumb man sat on the plinth of the north arcade in his leather apron, the lump of stone between his knees.

Tap. Tap. Tap.

'I think he made you choose me, Gilbert, because I stand still so much!'

The dumb man got quickly to his feet. Jocelin smiled at him.

'Of all the people connected with this thing, I must seem to do least, don't you think?'

The dumb man smiled doglike, and hummed with his empty mouth. Jocelin laughed back, delightedly, and nodded as if they shared a secret.

'Ask those four pillars at the crossways if they do nothing!'

The dumb man laughed and nodded back.

'Soon I shall go to pray. You may follow me there, sit quietly, and work. Bring a cloth with you for the chips and dust, or Pangall will sweep you out of the Lady Chapel like a leaf. We mustn't fret Pangall.'

Then there was another new noise. He forgot the dumb man and listened, with his head turned to one side. No, he said to himself, they can't have done it yet; it can't be true! So he hurried away into the south aisle where he could peer slantwise across the cathedral into the north transept. He stood by the corner of the Peverel chantry. He whispered with joy too deep for the open air.

'It's true. After all these years of work and striving. Glory be.'

For they were doing the unthinkable. I have walked by there for years, he thought. There was outside and inside, as clearly divided, as eternally and inevitably divided as yesterday and today. The smooth stone of the inside, patterned and traced with paint, the rough and lichened stuff of the outside; yesterday, or a Hail Mary ago, they were a quarter of a mile apart. Yet now the air

12

blows through them. They touch, those separated sides. I can see, as through a spyhole, right across the close to the corner of the chancellor's house, where perhaps Ivo is.

Courage. Glory be. It is a final beginning. It was one thing to let him dig a pit there at the crossways like a grave for some notable. This is different. Now I lay a hand on the very body of my church. Like a surgeon, I take my knife to the stomach drugged with poppy.

And his mind played for a while with the fancy of the drug, thinking that the thin sound of mattins was the slow breathing of the drugged body where it lay stretched on its back.

There were young voices on the other side of the chantry.

'Say what you like; he's proud.'

'And ignorant.'

'Do you know what? He thinks he is a saint! A man like that!'

But when the two deacons saw the dean looming over them, they fell to their knees.

He looked down, loving them in his joy.

'Now, now, my children! What's this? Backbiting? Scandal? Denigration?'

They bent their heads and said nothing.

'Who is this poor fellow? You should pray for him, rather. But there.'

So he seized two handfuls of curls and tugged them gently, turning up first one white face and then the other.

'Ask the chancellor for a penance concerning this matter. Understand the penance rightly, dear children, and it will be a great joy to you.'

He turned away from them, to walk up the south aisle;

13

but there was still another delay. Pangall stood at the temporary door that led through the wood and canvas screen from the south ambulatory into the crossways; and now, seeing Jocelin, he dismissed his attendant sweepers and limped forward, left foot dragging a little, broom held crossways in his hands.

'Reverend Father.'

'Not now, Pangall.'

'Please!'

Jocelin shook his head, and made to pass round; but the man held out a roughened hand as if he would dare to lay it on the dean's cassock. Jocelin stopped, looked down and spoke quickly.

'What d'you want, then? The same thing as before?'

'They —'

'They are not your business. Understand that once and for all.'

But still Pangall stood his ground, looking up under his thatch of dark hair. There was dust on his brown tunic, his crossgartered legs, his old shoes. There was dust on his angry face. His voice was hoarse, with dust and anger.

'The day before yesterday they killed a man.'

'I know. Listen, my son —'

Pangall shook his head with such solemnity and certainty, that Jocelin fell silent, looking down, mouth open. Pangall grounded the handle of his broom, and stood with his weight on it. He looked round the pavement, then up at the dean's face.

'One day, they will kill me.'

For a while they were both silent, among the singing that the echo made of the work noises. The dust danced in the sun between them. All at once Jocelin remembered his joy. He dropped both his

14

hands on the man's leather shoulders and gripped tight.

'They shan't kill you. No one shall kill you.'

'Then they will drive me out.'

'No harm shall come to you. I say so.'

Pangall gripped the broom fiercely. He put his weight on both feet. His mouth twisted.

'Reverend Father, why did you do it?'

Resignedly Jocelin let his hands fall and clasped them before his waist.

'You know as well as I do, my son. So that this House will be even more glorious than before.'

Pangall showed his teeth.

'By breaking the place down?'

'Now stop, before you say too much.'

When Pangall answered, it was like an attack.

'Have you ever spent the night here, Reverend Father?'

Gently, as to a little one.

'Many nights. You know that as well as I do, my son.'

'When snow falls and all that weight lies on the lead roof; when leaves choke the gutter —'

'Pangall!'

'My great-great-grandfather helped to build it. In the hot weather he would roam through the roof over the vault up there, as I do. Why?'

'Softly, Pangall, softly!'

'Why? Why?'

'Tell me then.'

'He found one of the oak logs smouldering. By the luck of his wit he carried an adze with him. If he went for water the roof would have been ablaze and the lead like a river before he could get back. He adzed out the

15

embers. He made a hole you could hide a, a child in; and he carried the embers out in arms that were roasted like pork. Did you know that?'

'No.'

'But I know it. We know it. All this —' And he made a jab with his broom at the dust-laden moulding — 'this breaking and digging up — let me take you into the roof.'

'I've other things to do and so have you.'

'I must speak with you —'

'And what d'you suppose you're doing now?'

Pangall took a step back. He looked round at the pillars and the high, glittering windows as if they could tell him what to say.

'Reverend Father. In the roof. Just by the door from the stair in the south-west turret there is an adze, sharpened, tallowed, guarded, ready.'

'That's well done. Wise.'

Pangall made a gesture with his free hand.

'It's nothing. It's what we are for. We've swept, cleaned, plastered, cut stone and sometimes glass, we've said nothing —'

'You've all been faithful servants of the House. I try to be one myself.'

'My father, and my father's father. And the more so since I'm the last.'

'She's a good woman and wife, my son. Hope and be patient.'

'They've made a game of my whole life. And more. It's not just this — Come and see my cottage.'

'I've seen it.'

'But not in the last few weeks. Come quickly —' and limping, hurrying with a beckoning hand, his broom trailing from the other, Pangall led the way into the

16

south transept. 'It was our place. What will become of us? There!'

He pointed through the little door into the yard that lay between the cloisters and the south aisle. Jocelin had to bow his skullcapped head to pass through it. He stood just inside the door with Pangall under his left shoulder, and he let his jaw drop at the work that had been done. The yard was full of stacks and piles of cut stone. They reached up to the windows between the buttresses. What space the stones left was filled with baulks of timber and the passage between them was no more than a catwalk. On the left of the entrance was a bench against the south wall, with a thatched cover. Glass, and lead strip was heaped up under the thatch, and two of the master builder's men were working there, chink, snip, snip.

'D'you see, Father? I can scarcely find my own door!'

Jocelin edged after him between the piles.

'This is all they've left me. And for how long, Father?'

In front of the cottage there was left a space no bigger than a chantry, and the wall at the end of it was puddled with slops. Jocelin looked curiously at the cottage since he had never been as close to it before. On earlier inspections, a courteous glance through the door into the yard had been sufficient; for when all was said, church property or not, the yard and the cottage was Pangall's kingdom. Daily the shadow of that cottage lay on the south east window — like a monument built against the architect's intentions. Now the substance of the cottage was close to his eye, another coming together of inside and out. The cottage hung in the angle of the yard against the cathedral wall, like the accretions under the eaves of an ancient house, where generations of swallows and sparrows have left their marks and the roots of nests. It was a building at once furtive, secret, and blatant; built without permission, tolerated, tacitly unmentioned, because the family that lived there was indispensable. It concealed one buttress and part of a window. Some of the wall was grey cathedral stone, and nearly as old as the stones of the cathedral itself. There was a paradoxical dripstone with no window to protect. Some of the wall was ancient beam, wattle and daub. There were wafer thin bricks older than the cottage or the cathedral, loot turned up in some cold harbour that the Romans had not seen for a thousand years. A bit of the roof was lapped most expensively in lead; another bit in slates that bore an absolute likeness to the slates roofing the kitchen of the Vicars Choral. Then there was thatch, but so decayed, it was nothing but a sloughed and weedy undulation. A dormer window had been shaped deliberately to take a rectangle of what looked like painted glass, no less; but the other window was smaller and filled with horn. After no more than a hundred and fifty years, the piecemeal construction gave the cottage an air of antiquity and fatigue. The whole thing sagged like the thatch, as though its random parts had slumped together in a position of final rest.

Jocelin looked at the cottage, glanced sideways at the piles of building material that crowded round it, one insolence attacking another.

'I see.'

Before he could say more, a voice began to sing sweetly in the cottage. Goody came out, saw him, stopped singing, smiled sideways and emptied a wooden bucket at the foot of the south wall. She went in again; and once more he heard her sing.

'Now Pangall. All these things you have said. We are

18

old friends, you and I, despite our different stations, so let's be practical. They will build, and that's the end of it. Tell me what's really the matter.'

Pangall looked quickly away at the men who were whistling and snapping glass. Jocelin leaned down.

'Is it your good wife? Do they work too near her?'

'Not that.'

Jocelin thought for a moment, nodding wisely at the man. He spoke softly.

'Do they treat her as some men will treat women in the street? Call after her? Speak lewdly?'

'No.'

'Then what?'

Anger had gone out of Pangall's face. There was a kind of puzzled pleading in it.

'It's this, when you come down to it. Why me? Isn't there anyone else? Why must they make a fool of me?'

'We must be patient.'

'All the time. Everything I do. They jeer and laugh. If I look behind me —'

'You're too thinskinned, man. You must put up with it.'

Pangall set his face.

'How long?'

'They'll be a trial to us all. I admit that. Two years.'

Pangall shut his eyes and groaned.

'Two years!'

Jocelin patted his shoulder.

'Now think, my son. The stones will go up bit by bit, and the wood. They won't be forever snapping glass in your face. Then the spire will be done and our House more wonderful still.'

'I shan't see it, Reverend Father.'

'Why not, in the name of —'

He stopped, aware of his sudden irritation; but then

19

as he looked at the man eye to eye, the irritation came back in a sudden flurry. For he saw the words in Pangall's head, as clearly as if they had been written there; *because there are no foundations, and Jocelin's Folly will fall before they fix the cross on the top.*

He set his teeth.

'You are like all the rest; not like the old man with the adze. You haven't any faith.'

But Pangall was looking down. He crept close in Jocelin's shadow. His dusty thatch, his brown and dung-colour and dust was six inches below Jocelin's face, and leaning inward, close to the cassock. Through his irritation, Jocelin heard a hoarse and private mutter.

'How can I bear it? They strike me where I haven't any guard. I'm ashamed before people, before my own wife; it adds up in here, and each day, each hour —'

There was a sharp tap on the instep of Jocelin's shoe; and as he looked he saw a wet star there with arms to it and tiny globes of water that slid off the dubbin into the mud of the yard. Impatiently, he let out his breath, and looked round for something to say. But the sunlight on stone drew his eye upward, to the empty air above the crossways, where the battlements of the stump tower waited for the master builder and his men. He remembered the workmen breaking up the pavement below the crossways and his irritation vanished in a return of excitement.

'Be patient I said! And I promise you this. I shall speak to the master builder.'

He patted the leather shoulder again and hurried away, edging between the piles of wood and stone. The workmen at the bench kept their backs to him. He ducked through the little door into the south transept, and stood for a moment, blinking in the dusty sunlight. He saw how paving slabs were piled to one side at the crossways, and how the two delvers stood over ankles below the floor. Beyond them in the north wall, a larger patch of the outworld was visible, so that he could see to the thatched shelter among the graves, where the treetrunks lay ready. He stood, smiling round his nose, head up, and he saw Adam Chaplain come hurrying towards him up the south aisle, with a letter in his hands; but he waved him aside.

'Later, dear man. When I have prayed.'

So he went quickly, smiling, with joy like wings, through the south ambulatory between the choir and the vestry. The service was over and there was no one about but two vicars choral, standing and talking by the inner door. In the Lady Chapel the priedieu had been set ready for him on the centre line. He bent to the altar then sank kneeling in the priedieu. Somewhere near, he could hear the dumb man begin to tap and scrape gently on stone. But he hardly had to put the thin noises away from him, since joy was its own prayer, and immediate to the heart.

What can I do on this day of days when at last they have begun to fashion my vision in stone, but give thanks?

Therefore with angels and archangels —

Joy fell on the words like sunlight. They took fire.

He had a tariff of knees. He knew how they should be after this length of kneeling or that. Now, when they had passed through a dull ache, to nothing, he knew that more than an hour had passed. He was in himself again; and as the slow lights swam before his closed eyes he felt the pain surge back in his shins and knees and thighs. My prayer was never so simple; that's why it took so long.

And then, quite suddenly, he knew he was not alone. It was not that he saw, or heard a presence. He felt it, like the warmth of a fire at his back, powerful and gentle at the same time; and so immediate was the pressure of that personality, it might have been in his very spine.

He bent his head in terror, hardly breathing. He allowed the presence to do what it would. I am here, the presence seemed to say, do nothing, we are here, and all work together for good.

Then he dared to think again, in the warmth at his back.

It is my guardian angel.

I do Thy work; and Thou hast sent Thy messenger to comfort me. As it was of old, in the desert.

With twain he covered his face, and with twain he covered his feet, and with twain he did fly.

Joy, fire, joy.

Lord; I thank Thee that Thou hast kept me humble!

Once more, the windows were coming together. The saint's life still burned in them with blue and red and green; but the spark and shatter of the sun had shifted. He was back, looking at the familiar window over clasped hands; and the angel had left him.

Tap. Tap. Tap.

Scrape.

Thou dost glorify the lives of Thy chosen ones, like the sun in a window.

He bore down on the desk and managed to break up the rigor of his knees. He tottered a step or two before he could stand and walk erect. He smoothed out his cassock with his right hand, and while he was doing this, he remembered the tap and scrape and looked towards the north wall, where the dumb man sat, his mouth hanging open. There was a cloth on the pavement at his feet, and he scraped carefully at the lump of stone. He stood up quickly when Jocelin's shadow fell on him. He was a hefty young man and he held the carving easily in both hands by his stomach. The joy and comfort and peace of the angel laid a favour on the young man's face as on all the world; so Jocelin felt a smile bend the seams of his own face as he looked round his nose at him. He was a big young man too; could look at the dean on a level, eye to eye. Jocelin looked him over, in the joy of the angel, still smiling, loving him, the brown face and neck, the chest where the laced leather parted to show a covert of black hair, the curly head, the black eyes under their black eyebrows, the brown arms sweated at the armpits through the jerkin, the legs crossbound, rough shoes white with dust.

'I was still enough for you today, I think!'

The young man nodded eagerly again and again, and made a humming noise in his throat. Jocelin went on smiling into the eager, doglike eyes. Where I led he would follow. If only he were the master builder! Perhaps one day —

'Show me, my son.'

The young man shifted a hand under the stone and held it in profile by his chest. Jocelin lifted his head and laughed down at it.

'Oh no, no no! I'm not as beaky as that! Not half as beaky!'

Then the profile caught his attention again and he fell silent. Nose, like an eagle's beak. Mouth open wide, lined cheeks, hollow deep under the cheekbone, eyes deep in their hollows; he put up a hand to the corner of his mouth and pulled at the parallel ridges of flesh and skin. He opened his mouth to feel how that action stretched them, striking his teeth together three times as he did so.

'And no, my son. I haven't as much hair as that either!'

The young man shot out his free arm sideways, brought it in again, and made the palm sweep through the air in a swallow flight.

'A bird? What bird? An eagle, perhaps? You are thinking of the Holy Spirit?'

Arm out again, sweeping.

'Oh I see! You want to get an impression of speed!'

Young man laughing all over his face, nearly dropping the stone but catching it again, communion over the stone as with an angel, joy —

Then silence, both looking at the stone.

Rushing on with the angels, the infinite speed that is stillness, hair blown, torn back, straightened with the wind of the spirit, mouth open, not for uttering rain-water, but hosannas and hallelujahs.

Presently Jocelin lifted his head, and smiled ruefully.

'Don't you think you might strain my humility, by making an angel of me?'

Humming in the throat, headshake, doglike, eager eyes.

'So this is how I shall be built in, two hundred feet up, on every side of the tower, mouth open, proclaiming day and night till doomsday? Let me see the face.'

The young man stood obediently, with the full face turned towards him. For a long time then, they were both still and silent, while Jocelin looked at the gaunt, lifted cheekbones, the open mouth, the nostrils strained wide as if they were giving lift to the beak, like a pair of wings, the wide, blind eyes.

It is true. At the moment of vision, the eyes see nothing.

'How do you know so much?'

But the young man looked back blank as the stone. Jocelin laughed a little again and patted the brown cheek then tweaked it.

'Your hands know, perhaps, my son. There's a kind of wisdom in them. That was why the Almighty tied your tongue.'

Humming in the throat.

'Go now. You can work at me again tomorrow.'

Jocelin turned away and stopped suddenly.

'Father Adam!'

He hurried across the Lady Chapel to where Adam Chaplain stood in the shadows under the south windows.

'Have you waited all this time?'

The little man stood patiently, the letter held in his hands like a tray. His colourless voice scratched itself into the air.

'I am under obedience, my Lord.'

'I am to blame, Father.'

But even as he said it, other things pushed the contrition out of his head. He turned and walked away towards the north ambulatory, hearing the click of nailed sandals behind him.

'Father Adam. Did you see — see anything behind me there, as I knelt?'

Creak of a mouse voice.

'No, my Lord.'

'If you had, of course, I should have commanded your silence.'

He stopped in the ambulatory. There were shafts and trunks of sunlight overhead; but the wall between the choir and the wide passage round it, kept the pavement where they stood, in shadow. He heard the noises of breaking stone from the crossways, and watched the dust that danced even here beyond the wooden screen, if

25

more slowly. This drew his eyes upward, to the high vaulting, and he stepped back to see it more clearly. He felt soft toes under his shod heel.

'Father Adam!'

But the little man said nothing, did nothing. He stood, still holding the letter, and there was not even a change of expression in his face; and this might be, thought Jocelin, because he has no face at all. He is the same all round like the top of a clothespeg. He spoke, laughing down at the baldness with its fringe of nondescript hair.

'I ask your pardon, Father Adam. One forgets you are there so easily!' And then, laughing aloud in joy and love — 'I shall call you Father Anonymous!'

The chaplain still said nothing.

'And now. About this foolish letter.'

On the other side of the church, the choir had gathered for the next service. He heard them begin the processional chant. They were moving; you could hear the children's voices first most clearly; then these faded, to be replaced by the low voices of the Vicars Choral. Presently these faded too, and from the Lady Chapel, a single voice sang, wah, wah, wah, wah, wah; and chased itself in echoes round the acreage of the vault.

'Tell me Father. Everyone knows, that as the world has these things, she is my aunt?'

'Yes, my Lord.'

'One must be charitable, as always — even to such as she is; or has been.'

Still silence. With twain he covered his feet. Thy angel is my security. I can bear anything now.

'What do they say?'

'It is tavern talk, my Lord.'

'Tell me, then.'

26

'They say that if it had not been for her wealth, you would never build the spire.'

'That's true. What else?'

'They say that even if your sins are as scarlet, money can buy you a grave next to the High Altar.'

'Do they so?'

The letter was still there, like a white tray. A faint perfume still clung round it and pushed out at the nostrils, so that the ambulatory, dark beneath its north windows, seemed invaded by a breath of artificial spring. For all the new beginning and the angel, his irritation came back.

'It stinks!'

The wah-wah-wah from the Lady Chapel died away.

'Read it out!'

' "To my nephew and —" '

'Louder.'

(And from the Lady Chapel, a single voice, slow, defeating the echo. I believe in one God.)

' "— father in God Jocelin, Dean of the cathedral church of the Virgin Mary." '

(And from the Lady Chapel, voices young and old chanting together. Of all things visible and invisible.)

' "This letter is written for me by Master Godfrey, since I suppose among your church business and building matters you neglected the ones he has written for me during these last three years. Well, dear nephew, here I am again, bringing up the old question. Can you not spare a word for me? It was a different and a much quicker answer you gave when the question was one of money. Let us be frank. I know and the world knows and you know, what my life has been. But all that ended with his death — murder, martyrdom, I should

say. The rest is penance before my Maker, who I hope
will vouchsafe his unworthy handmaid many more years
of living death to repent in." '

(Suffered under Pontius Pilate.)

' "I know you are silent because you condemn my
traffic with an earthly king. But is it not said render unto
Caesar the things which are Caesar's? I have done that at
least, to the best of my power. I was to lie in Winchester,
among the kings, I had his word for it, but they have
turned me away, though the time will soon come when
dead kings are all I am fit to lie among." '

(To judge the quick and the dead.)

' "Master Godfrey wishes to strike out that last sen-
tence, but I say he must leave it in. Are all the bones in
your church so sanctified? You may say I have small
prospect of heaven, but my hope is better. There is a
place, or there was before your day, on the south side of
the choir, where the sun comes in, between some old
bishop and the Provoste Chantry. I think the High
Altar could see me there and perhaps be more absent-
minded than you about those faults I still find it so difficult entirely to repent of." '

(The forgiveness of sins and the life everlasting.)

' "What is it? More money? Do you want two spires
rather than one? Well, you may as well know that I in-
tend to divide my fortune, he was generous in that as
in all else, between you and the poor, setting aside
sufficient for my tomb, a mass priest, a gift for the
cathedral in your dear mother's name, once we were
very close —" '

He reached out and folded the letter together in the
chaplain's hands.

'We could do well enough without women, Father
Anonymous. What do you think?'

'They have been called dangerous and incomprehensible, my Lord.'

(Amen.)

'And the answer, my Lord?'

But Jocelin was remembering the new beginning, remembering the angel, and the invisible lines of the spire that even now for those who knew, had sketched themselves in the sunny sky over the crossways.

'Answer?' he said, laughing. 'What need is there to change a decision? We shall make no answer.'

CHAPTER TWO

⟨~✶~⟩

He came out of the ambulatory through the temporary wooden door and stood blinking for a moment in the sudden light of the crossways. The gap in the wall of the north transept was big enough for a wagon; and some of the master builder's army were busy tidying the edges. The dust was thicker than ever, like yellow smoke, so that he coughed, and his eyes ran. The two men breaking up the pavement were working out of sight to their thighs, and the dust was so thick in that part of the air, he thought their faces were monstrously deformed, until he saw that they had drawn cloths over their mouths; and these cloths were caked with dust and sweat. A hodman stood waiting by the pit, and when he had a hodful he walked away through the north transept and another took his place. As the hodman came from more dust to less, with the hod over his shoulder, he began a laboured singing. Jocelin understood these words, and after the first few, he clapped his hands over his ears and opened his mouth in the dust to rebuke the singer, who paid no attention, but marched singing through the gap in the wall. Jocelin hurried into the nave and peered round him. He went poking and peering round pillars but found no one. He went purposefully through the south transept; he clashed the great cloister door, he wrenched back the curtain. But

30

there was no Principal Person in the scriptorium; only a deacon who compared two manuscripts, his nose three inches from the page.

'Where is the Sacrist?'

The young man leapt to his feet, saving a book as he did so.

'My Lord, he came through —'

Jocelin snatched the next curtain aside; but there was no one in the school room either. The benches were in disorder, one lying on its side. He went to the arcade of the cloister, leaned with both hands on the sill among the bone counters and game board scratched in the stone and stuck his head through. The Sacrist was sitting on a bench taken from the school room. He sat in the sun, his back against a pillar of the arcade, hands folded in his lap.

'Father Anselm!'

An early fly struck Father Anselm on the nose and bounced away. He opened his eyes without focusing, then he shut them again.

'My Lord Sacrist!'

Jocelin hurried through the next curtain, entered the central square, stood by Father Anselm, put by his irritation, and spoke in a normal, conversational voice.

'The nave is empty. No one is standing guard.'

Though he seemed asleep, Father Anselm was trembling very slightly. He opened his eyes but looked away.

'The dust, my lord. You know how it is with this poor chest of mine.'

'There was no need for you to sit there. You have authority!'

Anselm coughed delicately, tuh, tuh, tuh.

'How can I ask others to do what I can't do myself?

And after a day or two there will be less dust. The master builder told me so.'

'So meanwhile they can sing any filthy song they like?'

Despite his care, his determination, Jocelin's voice rose, and his right fist clenched. Deliberately he unclenched it, then flexed the fingers as if the gesture had meant nothing. But the Sacrist had seen, even though he now looked at the great cedar. He was still shaking, but his voice was calm.

'When you consider, my Lord Dean, to what a degree we must accept a disruption of our normal life, a song — forgive me — however worldly, seems an offence venial enough. After all, we have twelve altars in the side aisles of the nave. Because of this, this new building of ours, no candles burn there. And — forgive me again — but since these men, these strange creatures from every end of the world, seem willing to resort to violence at the slightest provocation, it might be wiser to let them sing.'

Jocelin opened his mouth and shut it silently. A picture of the grave deliberations in Chapter, flashed through his mind; but the Sacrist had turned from the cedar, and was looking straight at him, head on one side.

'Yes indeed, my lord Dean. Let them sing for a day or two, at least until the dust settles.'

Jocelin got his breath back.

'But we decided in Chapter!'

'I was given a certain latitude.'

'They defile the church.'

The Sacrist became motionless as the stones behind him. He no longer shook.

'At least they don't destroy it.'

Jocelin cried out.

'What d'you mean?'

The Sacrist's hands were still, as though he had forgotten how he had spread them.

'I, My Lord? Only what I said.'

Very carefully, the Sacrist brought in his hands and clasped them in his lap.

'You mustn't misunderstand me. It's conceivable that these ignorant men dirty the air with their words, just as they fill it with dust and stink. But they don't destroy the air. They don't destroy the building round it.'

'And I do!'

But the Sacrist was on guard.

'Who was talking about you, my Lord?'

'Ever since you voted against the spire in Chapter —'

The irritation in his throat stopped him. Anselm smiled slightly.

'A lamentable lack of faith, my Lord. I was overruled, and agree now, that we must all put our shoulders to the wheel.'

There was a hint of quotation round the wheel and the shoulder, so that the irritation in Jocelin's throat became anger.

'A lamentable lack of faith indeed!'

The Sacrist's smile was not only secure, but kind.

'We don't all feel ourselves so uniquely chosen, my Lord.'

'Do you think I don't see an accusation; however cautiously you phrase it?'

'I have said what I have said.'

'Sitting down.'

Some odd combination of causes was bringing Jocelin's blood to a rage. When he spoke again, there was a quick vibration in his voice.

'I believe our founder's statute is still valid.'

Now the Sacrist was very still. His delicate face was

33

perhaps a shade pinker. He put his feet back under him, and stood up slowly.

'My Lord.'

'The crossways still lack an overseer.'

The Sacrist said nothing. He clasped his hands, gave the merest inclination of his head, and turned to walk towards the cloister door. Suddenly Jocelin put out his hand.

'Anselm!'

The Sacrist stopped, turned, waited.

'Anselm, I didn't mean — You are the one friend I have left from the old days. Where have we come to?'

No answer.

'And you know I didn't mean you to leave like this. Forgive me.'

No smile under the eyes in the pink face.

'Of course.'

'There are a dozen people you could appoint. That boy in there, in the scriptorium. Surely Chrysostom can wait? Think how long he's been waiting!'

But the Sacrist was secure again, and shaking his head.

'I wouldn't ask anyone else to do it today. The dust, you know.'

Then they were both silent.

What am I to do? It is a small vexation and it will pass. But I am learning.

'Your command still stands, my Lord?'

Jocelin turned on his heel and looked up. He saw the arcade of the cloister and its battlements, inspected above them the buttresses and high windows of the south wall; followed up the angle between the wall and the transept to where the crossways were roofed briefly and squarely. The sunlight soaked the stone without warming it; and above the cliffs of stone, the sky was rinsed clear by a rainy night. It held no clouds, but a promise of wind. He let his eye rest on the invisible geometric lines that sketched themselves automatically above the battlements of the crossways, up there, where a bird wheeled, and drew to a point, four hundred feet up in the sky.

Let it be so. Cost what you like.

He looked back at the Sacrist, and surprised on his face an ambiguity of kindness and amused malice. I am your friend, said the smile, your confessor and your friend in particular. It said also, and in no way that could be answered; the invisible thing up there is Jocelin's Folly, which will fall, and in its fall, bury and destroy the church.

'Well, my Lord?'

Jocelin kept his voice low.

'Yes. Go, go.'

So the Sacrist clasped his hands and inclined his head. It was the perfect act of obedience; and it was more, because of the frayed thread that bound them. He paused at the door into the south transept; and Jocelin heard even in the delicate lifting of the latch and the careful pressure that grated back the door, an indefinable rebuke that was a sort of insolence, so that the thread snapped. Well, he thought, it is the end. Then he remembered how thick and long the thread had been, a rope binding them heart to heart, and his own was sore at the thought of it. And he knew that when he recovered from his irritation, he would grieve, remembering the cloister by the sea, the flashing water, the sun and sand.

'It's been coming for a long time.'

I didn't know how much you would cost up there, the four hundred feet of you. I thought you would cost no more than money. But still, cost what you like.

So he went back into the cathedral, and by the time he stood in the south transept, he had put Anselm out of his mind; for already there was less dust in the air, and what there was, hung diminishing. The delvers no longer worked with cloth over their mouths, nor was there a pillar of dust over them. Only their heads and the upthrown shovels were visible. When the shovels fell, they did not ring on rubble but cut with a soft scrape and chunk; and a hodman was carrying away a hodful of dark earth. But it was not the hodman or the delvers who interested him, for Roger Mason stood on the farther side of the pit, looking down, and his eyes were staring. He looked up for a moment at the pillars of the cross-ways, saw Jocelin without seeing him, and then stared down again. This was not new, for the master builder often looked at things without seeing them; and then again, he would look at a thing as if he could see nothing else, or hear or feel nothing else. He had the kind of eye on those occasions which seemed to grasp and mould what he looked at, or accept it in totality. But he was not looking like that now. He was looking down, eyes staring, and his swarthy face was full of sheer astonishment and disbelief. His blue hood was thrown back, to lie in folds round his thick neck, and he was passing a hand over his cropped, bullet head — feeling it as if he wanted to make sure it was there.

Jocelin stood on the lip of the pit and spoke to the master builder.

'Well, Roger? Are you satisfied?'

The master builder neither answered him nor looked at him. His hands were on his waist, thick legs astraddle, sturdy body in its brown tunic leaning forward a little. He spoke down the pit.

'Use the prod.'

One delver relaxed, and smeared a hand over his sweaty face. The other disappeared from sight and began to make grunting noises. The master builder knelt down quickly, his hands on the edge of a slab, and leaned still further forward.

'Anything?'

'Nothing, master. Come-hup!'

The man's head appeared and his two hands. He held the iron rod in both of them, one thumb marking a distance, the other on the shining point. The master builder inspected the rod slowly from one thumb to the other. He looked through Jocelin, shaped his lips to whistle but made no sound. Jocelin understood that he was ignored, and turned away to examine the nave. He caught sight of the white, noble head of Anselm where he sat two hundred yards away by the west door, obeying the letter of his instructions, but out of earshot and almost out of sight. Jocelin felt a sudden return of pain that the man should look like one thing and behave like another; a touch of astonishment too, and incredulity. If he wants to behave like a child, let him sit there till he grows to the stone! I shall say nothing.

He turned back to the master builder, and this time knew himself to be recognised.

'Well Roger my son?'

The master builder straightened up, knocked the dust from his knees, then brushed it from his hands. The delvers were at work again, scrape, chunk.

'Did you understand what you saw, reverend father?'

'Only that the legends are true. But then; legends are always true.'

'You priests pick and choose.'

You priests.

I must be careful not to anger him, he thought. As

long as he does what I want, let him say what he likes.

'Confess, my son. I told you the building was a miracle and you would not believe me. Now your eyes have seen.'

'Seen what?'

'A miracle. You've seen the foundations; or rather, the lack of them.'

There was contempt and amusement in the master builder's laugh.

'The foundations are there. They are just about enough for a building of this weight. Look, you can see what they did. Follow the side of the pit down. Rubble down to there, and then something more; then nothing but mud. They made a raft of brushwood and piled the filling on top. And even that isn't certain. There must be gravel under here somewhere, and it must come near the surface; *must* come near the surface, or I don't know my business. Perhaps there was a bank, a reef the river left. That mud down there may be no more than a pocket of dirt.'

Jocelin laughed down over his nose delightedly. His chin lifted.

'Yet your craft can find nothing certain, my son. You say they built a raft. Why not believe the building floats on it? It's simpler to believe in a miracle.'

The master builder examined him silently, until he had finished laughing.

'Come over here where we can talk together. Now. Say, if you like, that the building floats. It is a manner of speaking. It may be so —'

'It *is* so, Roger. We have always known it. Perhaps next time, you will believe me. This excavation was quite unnecessary.'

'I'm digging the hole because of my workmen.'

'Your army? I thought you were their general!'

'Sometimes the army does the leading.'

'That's a poor sort of general, Roger.'

'Look. The foundations, the raft if you like, are just about enough for the building. But for nothing more; or little more. And now these workmen know it.'

Despite his attempts at solemnity, a kindly amusement came out in Jocelin's voice.

'Didn't you dig the pit for me, too, Roger? A pit to catch a dean?'

But Roger Mason was not smiling. He was looking across under his heavy eyebrows like a bull.

'What d'you mean?'

'Let the dean see how impossible the spire is. There's no work this summer at Winchester or Chichester, Lacock, Christchurch, no abbeys to build, no nunneries or priories; and the new king isn't a castle builder. But here, you thought, we can tide the summer over, show dean Jocelin what a fool he is. That way, you can keep the army together until something turns up, because without the army you're nothing.'

The master builder was smiling a little now.

'If I find gravel soon, reverend Father, then we can think again. Otherwise —'

'Otherwise you'll agree to build a squat tower, carefully, timidly, one eye asquint to see the building doesn't sink? How clever you think you are! A tower can be cut off at any height, can't it, Roger? So your army can winter here, and murder more people.'

'I lost my best stonecutter in that fight.'

'And all for a squat tower. No, Roger.'

'I'm looking for gravel. That's a real foundation, is gravel.'

But Jocelin was nodding and smiling at him.

'You'll see how I shall thrust you upward by my will. It's God's will in this business.'

The master builder had stopped smiling. He spoke angrily.

'If they had intended a spire they'd have laid the foundations for it!'

'They intended one.'

This time, he had all Roger Mason's interest.

'Plans?'

'What plans?'

'The whole building — you've seen them? You have them in the archives?'

Jocelin shook his head.

'There aren't any plans, my son. Such men as they were needed nothing drawn out on sheepskin, or marked on a board. But I know what they intended.'

The master builder scratched his head, then beckoned.

'Come with me, reverend Father, and examine the pillars.'

'I know them well enough. Remember this is my house, under God.'

'But see them the way I see them myself.'

There were four pillars at the corners of the crossways. They rose, each a cluster of stems that splayed out in branches to support the roof. There was a dimness under the roof, so that from a hundred and twenty feet below it, the eye was unable to follow the pattern round the wooden lid that closed the vent in the centre. The master builder went to the pillar at the south west corner and smacked one of the stems with his palm. The stone was too smooth to hold dust; and a distorted hand shot out to meet the one he put on the surface.

'Do they seem thick and strong to you, father?'

'Immense.'

'But see how thin they are for their length!'

'It's their beauty.'

'They support nothing but the roof; and they were never intended to bear much more than their own weight.'

Jocelin lifted his chin.

'Nevertheless, they must be strong enough.'

The master builder's smile was ambiguous as the Sacrist's had been.

'How would you set about building one of these pillars, reverend Father?'

Jocelin went to the pillar and peered closely at it. Each pipe in the cluster was thicker than a man's body. He passed his fingers down the surface of one.

'There. You see? These horizontal cracks, seams; what do you call them? Joists? They must have cut slices and then piled them, as children playing at checkers will pile one counter on another.'

Now there was a grimness in the master builder's smile.

'You say they were good men, reverend Father; and perhaps they were honest. But there are other ways than that.'

Pangall came limping through the crossways. Behind him a hodman limped in silent imitation. He had the very lurch and sidle, the carriage of the head, even the raging look. Pangall swung round, and the hodman stopped, to burst into a cackle of laughter. Pangall passed muttering into his kingdom.

'Now Roger, we shall speak of something else. That man —'.

'Pangall?'

'He's a very faithful servant. Tell your men to leave him alone.'

Silence.

'Roger?'

'The man's a fool. Can't he take a joke?'

'It's a stale one by now, whatever it is.'

The master builder looked stonily at the door into Pangall's kingdom and said nothing.

'Roger. Why must they pick on him?'

The master builder looked quickly at Jocelin. All at once there was a kind of mental jolt between them, like a wheel taking a rut; and Jocelin felt the fluttering of a dozen things behind his lips that he might have given sound to, if it had not been for the dark eyes looking so directly into his. It was like standing on the edge of something.

'Roger?'

But a small congregation was returning from the Lady Chapel, down the north ambulatory, with Rachel giving tongue at their head. The fluttering speeches died away.

'Why *do* they?'

Roger Mason had turned back to the pit.

'It's our way of keeping off bad luck.'

Then Rachel had broken away from the rest and was hurrying across the pavement to them, talking and gesticulating before she was properly within reach — 'Didn't expect their foundations to be dug up before Doomsday and why not, after all they must have been under contract like my man here —' talking and nodding, body shaken with vehemence, skirt not held up but clutched up until one saw too much of a clumsy ankle and foot — 'Birchwood under the rubble was what you expected, wasn't it Roger? He always knows, my Lord'

— My Lord as if she were not a woman but a canon with a valid vote in chapter! Her whole body a part of speech, black eyes popping, not like a decent, reticent English-woman (not like silent Goody Pangall, my dear daughter-in-God) but even pretending to knowledge, building knowledge, even contradicting a man! Rachel, dark haired, dark eyed and energetic, with her constant flow, she, earth's most powerful argument for celibacy if one was wanted — 'Forgive me my Lord but I must say it, I know a little about these things; I remember what Roger's old master said. "Child —" he called me child, you see because Roger was his assistant then — "Child, a spire goes down as far as it goes up —" or was it "Up as far as it goes down"? But what he meant you see was —' and then she leaned her head on one side, smiling mysteriously, one finger sticking in Jocelin's face '— was that there has to be as much weight under a building as there is over it. So if you are going up four hundred feet you will have to go down four hundred feet. Isn't that so Roger? Roger?' On and on she went, released from the necessary, the penitential silence of the service, her body and her dark face shaken by the words as a pipe is shaken by the water that jets out of it. Yet there was a curious thing about Roger and Rachel Mason. Not only were they inseparable, but alike in appearance; more like brother and sister than man and wife, dark, sturdy, redlipped. They were islanded, and their life was a pattern of its own. Roger never struck her, and their frequent quarrels were like flares, blown out presently by some wind, to leave the scene just as it had been before. They revolved round each other in a way which people found incomprehensible. It was impossible to understand how they put up with each other; though certain techniques of living could be observed in them.

For example, Roger Mason had evolved a method of dealing with Rachel which often made farce of a situation, as it did now. He ignored her, merely raising his voice, so that he could be heard and understood. This never seemed to irritate him; but it was certain to irritate the third in the party, especially when the third was a high dignitary of the church.

'— a much more complicated problem than you think.'

And Rachel, face shaken now, so the master builder's words were obscured again. Jocelin raised his own voice, consenting to the farce, and angered by it.

'We were talking of Pangall!'

'Such a sweet thing, and such a pity she has no children but then neither have I, my Lord, we must bear this cross!'

'— will build as high as I can —'

'— as high as you dare —'

Suddenly Jocelin heard his voice in clear, with nothing to fight against. Rachel had turned away. Her torrent was falling into the pit which swallowed it.

'And what is the good of a small dare, Roger? My dares are big ones!'

'Well?'

'Four hundred feet of dare!'

'I haven't convinced you then.'

Jocelin smiled at him, but nodded meaningly.

'Start to build. That's all I ask.'

They looked at each other, each determined, neither saying more, but aware that nothing had been settled, and this was only a truce. I will urge him up stone by stone, if I have to, thought Jocelin. He has no vision. He is blind. Let him think he can cut off a tower where he likes — but then Rachel turned back from the pit and they heard how little light there was in it now and how tired the men were, you can drive a willing horse just so far, they ought to knock off. So Jocelin turned away, furious with himself, and with the foolish woman, and with the man who was more easily able to ignore her than control her. He saw, with surprise, how the sun now came through the west windows; and with the sight he felt a pang of hunger. This made him angry too; and he was only slightly soothed to hear behind him the master builder bawl at Rachel.

'How can you be so *stupid*?'

Yet he knew that the roar was nothing, not even a rebuke, but perhaps something to keep off the bad luck, and that another five minutes would find them revolving round each other, laughing, or walking scandalously arm-in-arm; or muttering in some secret conversation that was no one else's business. And she was a good woman, as these things go; in all the rumoured and outrageous combinations of the sexes that were said to take place in New Street where the builders had set up camp, there was no scandal that touched either Rachel or the master builder. He looked down the nave into the sunlight, and found himself irritated again. The day began in joy, he thought; and great things have happened; there is a beginning, and there is my angel; and at the same time there is a diminution of joy, as if my angel were sent not only to strengthen and console me, but also as a warning. He saw father Anselm far off, sitting nobly by the west door, and the stillness of the old man under his crown of silver hair touched him with sorrow as well as irritation. He lifted his chin, and spoke to the preaching patriarchs in the clerestory.

'Let him sulk, if he wants to.'

45

Behind him, he heard laughter going out of the north transept through the new gap in the wall. Rachel was gone then; and he turned back for a moment to watch the master builder talking to the men by the pit. He wondered for a moment whether he should return and apply more pressure. I should not have gone to see him, he thought. I should have called him before me and rebuked him for the fight at the gate. What if the mayor demands a court? I didn't say the half of what I meant to say. It's that woman with her torrent, and her bold, shaken face. There are some women who are stronger than gates and bars by their very ignorance. I should rebuke her too for her presumption, teach her to know her place. Next time I see her without him, I will speak to her gently, and explain what she should be.

'Lord, what instruments we have to use!'

He heard the clicking of nailed sandals in the nave and knew it was the clothespeg man. He turned to watch. Father Adam was walking at his usual pace, neither slow nor fast, but as though he never did any thing else, only went like this from one day to the next, delivering, taking away, waiting for instructions, impersonal, without animation or complaint. Now he stood before his master, hands together, a doll a child might cut, the face too complex for an attempt, the arms, the hair painted on. He stood between Jocelin and the long-delayed meal with more business in his hands.

'Couldn't you wait, Father Adam?'

Father Anonymous.

Father Anonymous scratched an answer into the air with his useful voice.

'I thought you would wish to read it at once, my Lord.'

Jocelin sighed, and answered him, tired, irritable, and strangely sapped of joy.

'Let me see it, then.'

He turned to the east, held up the letter so that the sunlight fell on it. As he read, his face cleared, went from irritation, to satisfaction; then to delight.

'You did well to show it to me!'

He fell down on his knees, crossed himself and gave thanks. But the tide of joy was back, stood him on his feet, hurried him to where the master builder was talking to Jehan, his assistant, by the pit. As he came near, the master builder looked away from Jehan and spoke to him.

'They've found no gravel yet. And if the floods still rise we may have to wait for weeks before we can dig any deeper. Perhaps for months.'

Jocelin tapped the letter.

'Here's your answer, my son.'

'That?'

'My Lord Bishop has remembered us. Even though he kneels before the Holy Father at Rome, he remembers his distant sheep.'

The master builder answered impatiently.

'You never understand what I say, do you? I tell you, money can't build your spire for you. Build it of gold and it would simply sink deeper.'

Jocelin shook his head, laughing.

'Now I shall tell you, and then you can sleep easy. He sent no money. For what is money after all? But far, far, oh infinitely more valuable —' a tide of emotion swept Jocelin up so that his voice rose with it. He laid an arm across the master builder's shoulders and hugged him. 'We shall put this in the very topmost stone of the spire, and it will stand till the last day. My Lord Bishop is sending us a Holy Nail.'

He took his arm from the inscrutable master builder

and looked down the nave into the sun. He saw the white head of Father Anselm and knew at once that life was unendurable without the oil of healing. He went, almost at a run, down the nave towards the old man, and he waved the letter in his hand.

'Father Anselm!'

This time, father Anselm got up and stood. He did it slowly, bearing his martyrdom; and as if to complete the brave picture, he swallowed his three coughs so that they were only just audible. His face was cold and blank.

'Father Anselm. Friendship is a precious thing.'

Still blank. Buoyed up by his joy, Jocelin tried again.

'What have we done to it?'

'Is that a real question, my Lord, or a rhetorical one?'

Jocelin surrounded him with love.

'Would you like to read this letter?'

'Do you command me, my Lord?'

Jocelin laughed aloud.

'Anselm! Anselm!'

Stubbornly, the old man resisted his love, looked away towards the wood and canvas screen; coughed quietly but audibly, tuh, tuh, tuh.

'If it concerns the Chapter, my Lord, no doubt we shall all get to hear it in time.'

'Anselm. Here is a gift from me to you. I release you from this duty. I ought to have understood, that with all the opposition, and your health — There is no one, after all, engaged as I am to this business. I shall take it into my hands. You know that, and you know why, you of all people, my confessor, manager of my soul.'

'Let me see this clearly, my Lord. I am neither to be overseer, nor organise the overseers?'

'That's what I said.'

Anselm never altered his face. He kept his noble profile looking to the east, under the crown of white hair. He stood, senatorial, august and secure. The words fell.

'In writing?'

They fell. They were not jewels or pearls, as befitted the saintly face. They were pebbles. There was no insult, nothing to grasp; for if the words had insolence in them, they were nevertheless correct and according to the statute. *When it is ordained that a matter shall be so decided between two of the four Principal Persons, let it be written* — As if the statute hung there legibly in the air between them, Anselm clinched the matter by quoting from it.

'*What has been written, if there is a change, let that also be written; and let the small bone seal be affixed in the presence of two Persons.*'

'I know.'

Anselm spoke again, calmly and coldly. His cough had gone.

'Is that all, my Lord?'

'That's all.'

He heard the sacrist's steps going away up the nave, and he stood so, looking back over his left shoulder. I must erase him, he thought. I was deceived. He drops nothing but pebbles out of that noble head of his.

He looked down at the bishop's letter. It's like a pair of scales in the market, he thought. Joy carries me up in one pan, and Anselm sinks in the other. There is the Nail and my angel. There is the chancellor and the master builder and his wife.

Suddenly he understood how the wings of his joy were clipped close, and anger heated him again. Let them fall and vanish, so the work goes on! And as he passed under the west window, the letter clutched in one hand to his chest, he was muttering fiercely over his lifted chin.

'Now I must change my confessor!'

That night, when he knelt by his bed to pray before sleeping, his angel returned and stood at his back in a cloud of warmth, to comfort him a little.

CHAPTER THREE

꧁∽꧂

W hen he woke at dawn next morning, he could hear the rain, and he remembered what the master builder had said. So he prayed among other things for fine weather. But the rain came for three days, with only a half day to follow it of low cloud and soaked air; so that housewives hung what linen there was to wash before smouldering fires that dirtied more linen than they dried; and then there was wind and rain for a week. When he came out of his deanery, cloaked for the hurried passage to the cathedral, he would see the clouds at roof level so that even the battlements of the roof were blurred by them. As for the whole building itself, the bible in stone, it sank from glorification to homilectics. It was slimy with water streaming down over moss and lichen and flaking stones. When the rain drizzled, then time was a drizzle, slow and to be endured. When the rain lashed down, then the thousand gargoyles — and now men thought how their models mouldered in the graveyards of the Close or the parish churches — gave vent. They uttered water as if this were yet another penalty of damnation; and what they uttered joined with what streamed down glass and lead and moulding, down members and pinnacles, down faces and squared headlands to run bubbling and clucking in the gutter at the foot of the wall. When the wind came, it did not clear the sky, but cuffed the air this way and that, a bucketful of water with every cuff, so that even a dean must stagger, pushed from behind; or leaning against a gust like a blow, find his cloak whipped out like wings. When the wind fell, the clouds fell too and he could no longer see the top half of the building; and because of the drizzle he lost the sense of the size of it. Therefore the approaching eye had to deal with a nearer thing, some corner of wet stone, huge in detail and full of imperfections, like a skin seen too close. The reentrants on the north side — but there was no direction of light to show which was north and which south — stank with the memories of urination. The flood waters by the river, spread over the causeway, took no account of the guards at the city gate, but invaded the greasy streets. Men and women and children crouched by what fire they had and the smoke from damp logs or peat formed a haze under every roof. Only the alehouses prospered.

At the crossways of the cathedral there was no more digging. One day, Jocelin stood by the master builder, watched him lower a candle on a string, and saw how water shone at the bottom of the pit. Also, he smelt the pit, and recoiled from it. But the master builder took no account of smells. He stayed where he was, staring gloomily down at the candle. Jocelin became anxious and urgent. He hung by Roger Mason's shoulder.

'What will you do now, my son?'

Roger Mason grunted.

'There's plenty to do.'

He eased himself carefully into the bottom of a corkscrew stair and climbed out of sight; and later, Jocelin heard him moving carefully, a hundred and twenty feet up, by the vaulting.

It seemed to Jocelin that his first whiff of the pit began something new. Now he noticed how everywhere in the cathedral, the smell of stale incense and burnt wax had been joined by this more unpleasant odour. For the water, with guessed-at stealth, had invaded the graves of the great on either side of the choir or between the arcades of the nave. He found he was not the only one who noticed. The living, who made a profession of contempt for life, found this reminder too immediate, and conducted the services with faces of improper disgust. As he came from the Lady Chapel through the crossways — and nowadays they were dark — he would tell himself urgently; 'Here, where the pit stinks, I received what I received, all those years ago, and I fell on my face. It is necessary always, to remember.'

During this time, the master builder and some of his army worked in the roof over the crossways. They broke up the vaulting so that now if there was any light at all in the crossways and you looked up, you could see rafters. While some men worked there, disappearing into the corkscrew stairs that riddled the walls of the building, to appear later flysize in the triforium, others built scaffolding round the south-east pillar of the crossways. They set ladders from level to level, a spidery construction so that when it was finished the pillar looked like a firtree with the branches cut back. This new work was not without advantage to the services, for the builders could not be heard so easily in the roof. There was little more interruption to the stinking peace of the nave than the occasional blow of a maul at roofheight. Presently ropes began to hang down from the broken vault over the crossways, and stayed there, swinging, as if the building sweating now with damp inside as well as out, had begun to grow some sort of gigantic moss. The ropes were waiting for the beams that would be inched through the gap in the north wall; but they looked like moss and went with the smell. In this dark and wet, it took even Jocelin all his will, to remember that something important was being done; and when a workman fell through the hole above the crossways, and left a scream scored all the way down the air which was so thick it seemed to keep the scream as something mercilessly engraved there, he did not wonder that no miracle interposed between the body and the logical slab of stone that received it. Father Anselm said nothing in chapter; but he saw from the Sacrist's indignant stare how this death had been added to some account that one day would be presented. A dark night had not descended on the cathedral, but a midday without sun and therefore blasphemously without hope. There was hysteria in the laughter of the choir boys when the chancellor, tottering at the end of their procession from the vestry, turned left as he had done for half his life, instead of right to go into the Lady Chapel. Despite this laughter, these sniggers, the services went on, and business was done; but as in the burden of some nearly overwhelming weight. Chapter was testy, songschool was dull or fretful and full of coughing, and the boys quarrelled without knowing why. Little boys cried for no reason. Big boys were heavy eyed from nightmares of noseless men who floated beneath the pavements, their flat faces pressed against a heavy lid. So it was no wonder that the boys were ready to snigger at the chancellor. But one day, when he turned left, he kept going; and at last two of the vicars choral went after him. They found him in the semidark, pawing at the wooden screen between him and the crossways; and when they got him into the light, they saw how widely his right hand shook and how his face was empty. Then the ancient chancellor was removed to his house, and an extra terror of senility fell on the older men. Day and night acts of worship went on in the stink and halfdark, where the candles illuminated nothing but close haloes of vapour; and the voices rose, in fear of age and death, in fear of weight and dimension, in fear of darkness and a universe without hope.

'Lord, let our cry come unto Thee!'

Then there was a rumour of plague in the city. The number of faces — the strained, silent, shining-eyed faces before the light that betokened the presence of the Host — increased to a crowd. But Jocelin never joined them, since his own angel sometimes came to comfort, warm and sustain him. But like a good general, he saw how they needed help; for even to him, his instruments, these people he had to use, seemed little more than apes now that clambered about the building. He had the model of the cathedral brought to the crossways and stood against the north west pillar, spire and all, to encourage them. The model stood on a trestle table, and seemed the only clean thing in the building, though a finger that touched it came away wet.

That way, Christmas passed. Let the heavens rejoice, and let the earth be glad before the face of the Lord; because he cometh.

And it was supposed that he came; but the clouds still hung over the battlement; and if the drizzle ceased for a time, men looked up, feeling their cheek, and thinking that something was wrong. Once, when the rain had stopped, but the cavern of the nave was particularly noisome, Jocelin stopped by the model, to encourage himself. He detached the spire with difficulty, because the wood was swollen, and held the thing devoutly, like a relic. He caressed it gently, cradling it in his arms, and

55

looking at it all over, as a mother might examine her baby. It was eighteen inches long, squared for half its length and with tall windows, then bursting into a grove of delicate pinnacles, from among which the great spire rose, undecorated and slender with a tiny cross at the top. The cross was smaller than the one he wore hanging from his neck. He stood by the north west pillar, still cradling the spire, and telling himself that surely by now the floods must begin to sink. For there had been no rain for a week, though March was proving not windy, but dull. Even so, it was possible to believe that somewhere a soaked sun was struggling to reach the pocked mud of the fields. He stroked the spire, and heard Jehan talking himself out of the gap in the north transept. He shut his eyes, and thought to himself; we have endured! Let this be the turn of things! And it seemed to him behind his shut eyes as if he might feel the dry days gathering momentum, moving towards the light. He heard the maul sounds from the roof, and all at once he was excited by the thing in his arms; and the remembered lines drawing together in the air over the cathedral caught him with excitement by the throat. He felt life. He lifted his chin, opened his eyes and his mouth and was about to give thanks.

Then he stood still, saying nothing.

Goody Pangall had come out of Pangall's kingdom. She had come briskly for three steps. She stopped, and went back a step. She came forward more slowly towards the crossways but she was not looking at it. She was looking sideways. One hand gripped the cloak by her throat, and the other rose, bringing the basket with it. She was looking sideways as if she were sidling past a bull or a stallion. Her feet took her outside the scope of the tether, shoulder almost scraping the wall; only they were feet without much will to go forward. Her eyes were two black patches in her winter pallor, her lower lip had dropped open, and she would have looked foolish if anything so sweet could ever look foolish, and if it had not been for the open terror in her face. Drawn by the terror, Jocelin looked where she was looking; and now time moved in jerks, or was no time at all. Therefore it was not surprising that he found himself knowing what she was looking at, even before he saw the master builder.

Roger Mason had one foot on the bottom rung of the bottom ladder of the scaffolding round the south east pillar. He had come down from it, looking at Goody. He was turning. He was walking across the pavement, and she was creeping more and more slowly by the wall. She was shrinking too, shrinking and looking up sideways. He had her pinned there, he was looking down and talking earnestly, and she was still staring, her mouth open, and shaking her head.

A strange certainty fell on Jocelin. He knew things, he saw things. He saw this was one encounter of many. He saw pain and sorrow. He saw — and it was in some mode like that of prayer that he saw it — how the air round them was different. He saw they were in some sort of tent that shut them off from all other people, and he saw how they feared the tent both of them, but were helpless. Now they were talking earnestly and quietly; and though Goody shook her head again and again, yet she did not go, could not go, it seemed, since the invisible tent was shut round them. She held the basket in her hands, she was dressed for a visit to the market, she had no business to be talking to any man, let alone the master builder; she need do no more than shake her head, if that; she could easily ignore the man sturdy in his leather hose, brown tunic and blue hood, no there was no need even to pause; only need to pass by with head averted, for his hand was not on her. But she stood looking up at him sideways while her black, unblinking eyes and her lips, said no. Then suddenly she did indeed break away as if she would break physically something in the air: but uselessly for the invisible tent that made a pair of them expanded and kept ahead of her. She was still inside, would always be inside, even as she was inside now, hurrying away down the south aisle, her cheek no longer white, but red. Roger Mason stood looking after her down the south aisle as though nothing and no one in the whole world mattered, as though he could not help her mattering and was tormented by her mattering. He turned away, his back to Jocelin, as the north west door clashed behind Goody, he went to the ladder like a man sleepwalking.

Then an anger rose out of some pit inside Jocelin. He had glimpses in his head of a face that drooped daily for his blessing, heard the secure sound of her singing in Pangall's Kingdom. He lifted his chin, and the word burst out over it from an obscure place of indignation and hurt.

'No!'

All at once it seemed to him that the renewing life of the world was a filthy thing, a rising tide of muck so that he gasped for air, saw the gap in the north transept and hurried through it into what daylight there was. Immediately he heard the distant jeering of men, workmen; and at that temperature of feeling, understood what an alehouse joke it must seem to see the dean himself come hurrying out of a hole with his folly held in both hands. He turned again and rushed back into the crossways. But a little procession was coming up the north aisle; and there was Rachel Mason among them, carrying a dear bundle; so he spoke, giving her mechanically a congratulation and a blessing until the constable's lady snatched the baby away and swelled on towards the lady chapel and the christening. This left him with Rachel who was somehow compelled to stay behind; and though his eyes were blinded by the vision of Roger and Goody Pangall, he began to hear why. Nor could he believe how any woman, even an outraged one (her eyes bulging, tresses of black hair escaped across her cheek) would ever talk so. What paralysed him was not her spate, but the matter of it. Rachel, face shaken like a windowpane in a gale, was explaining to him why she had no child though she had prayed for one. When she and Roger went together, at the most inappropriate moment she began to laugh — *had* to laugh — it wasn't that she was barren as some people might think and indeed had said, my Lord, no indeed! But she *had* to laugh and then he *had* to laugh —

He stood in sheer disbelief and confusion, until she took herself away into the north ambulatory to catch up with the christening. He stood at the foot of the scaffolding, and part of the nature of woman burned into him; how they would speak delicately, if too much, nine thousand nine hundred and ninety-nine times; but on the ten thousandth they would come out with a fact of such gross impropriety, such violated privacy, it was as if the furious womb had acquired a tongue. And of all women in the world, only she, impossible, unbelievable, but existent Rachel would do it — no, be *forced* to do it by some urgency of her spatelike nature, to the wrong person, in the wrong place, at the wrong time. She stripped the business of living down to where horror and farce took over; particoloured Zany in red and yellow, striking out in the torture chamber with his pig's bladder on a stick.

He spoke viciously to the model in his hands.

'The impervious insolence of the woman!'

Then Zany struck him in the groin with the pig's bladder so that he jerked out a laugh that ended in a shudder.

He cried out loud.

'Filth! Filth!'

He opened his eyes and heard his own words ringing through the crossways. And there was Pangall with his broom, standing startled by the temporary door from the north ambulatory. So in a half-conscious effort to make his words logical and to hide their true source, Jocelin cried out again.

'The place is filthy dirty! They dirty everything!'

But men were coming through the crossways, Mel, the old stonecutter, and Jehan the chosen assistant to Roger Mason. He was laughing now as they passed Jocelin without paying any attention to him.

'Call her a wife? She's his keeper!'

So Jocelin, the blood still beating in his head, tried to speak naturally to Pangall, and found himself as breathless as if he had run the length of the cathedral.

'How is it with you now, Pangall my son?'

But Pangall was glaring belligerently from some private trouble or encounter of his own.

'How should it be?'

Jocelin went on in a nearly normal voice.

'I spoke to the master builder. Have you come to terms with them?'

'I? Never. You spoke a true word, reverend father. They dirty everything.'

'Do they leave you alone?'

Pangall answered him flatly.

'They'll never leave me alone. They've chosen me to be their fool.'

To keep off bad luck. His mouth repeated old words, as feet will take their own accustomed path.

'We work with what we have. We must all put up with them.'

But Pangall, who had moved away, swung round.

'Then why didn't you use *us*, father? I and my men —'

'You couldn't do it.'

Pangall opened his mouth to speak, then shut it again. He stayed where he was, peering fiercely at Jocelin; and there was a twitch at the corner of his mouth, that in anyone less devoted and faithful, would have been a sneer; and in the air between them, hung the words unspoken: and neither will they be able to do it, no one can do it. Because of the mud and the floods and the raft and the height and the thin pillars. It is impossible.

'They are a trial to us all, my son. I admit it. We must be patient. Didn't you say once that this is your house? There was sinful pride in that, but also loyalty and service. Never think you aren't understood and valued, my son. Presently they will go. In God's good time you will have sons —'

Pangall's sneer disappeared.

'The house they will have to guard and cherish will be far more glorious than this one. Think, man. In the middle of it this will stand up —' and passionately he held out the spire — 'and they will tell their children in their turn; "This thing was done in the days of our father." '

Pangall crouched. He held his broom crossways and it quivered. His eyes stared and the skin was drawn back

61

from his gleaming teeth. For a moment he stood like that, staring at the spire held out to him so enthusiastically. Then he looked up under his eyebrows.

'Do *you* make a fool of me too?'

He turned and limped quickly away into the south transept, and the slamming of the door into his kingdom echoed round the cathedral.

A maulman was working in the roof, bang, bang, bang. All at once the noise of the slamming and the banging, the smells, the memories, the tides of unspeakable feeling seemed to engulf Jocelin so that he gasped for air. He knew where there was air to be had, and his feet took him there, stumbling, till he fell on his knees before the quiet light on the altar. He stared at it, mouth open and yearning.

'I didn't know.'

Yet the purity of the light was out of reach, seemed a tiny door at an infinite distance. He knelt there, in the tide, and his mind was adrift in it, so that without knowing how the change had come about, he found himself looking down at the tiles of the floor with their heraldic beasts. Nearer to him than the floor were the people, the four of them — and his body shuddered again — Roger and Rachel Mason, Pangall and his Goody, like four pillars at the crossways of the building.

Then the shuddering lifted his head so that he was staring at the dully rich story of the window and the light of the altar was a divided thing, a light in each eye.

He whispered.

'Therefore Thou didst send Thy Angel to strengthen me.'

But there was no angel; only the tides of feeling, swirling, pricking, burning — a horror of the burgeoning evil thing, from birth to senility with its ghastly and complex strength between.

'Thou! Thou!'

The lights came together at an infinite distance and he yearned at the door. But the four people were dancing and clamoring in place of the angel at his back, so that the lights slid apart again. Then there were only two people, she and he in the tent, but now overwhelmed by a torrent of his sorrow and indignation so that he shut his eyes and groaned for his dear daughter.

Strengthen her O Lord, through Thy great mercy, and give her peace —

Then the thought leapt into his mind like a live thing. It was put there, as surely as the thrust of a spear. One moment his eyes were shut, his heart melted and adrift with sorrow. The next, and his mind was empty of all feeling, empty of everything but the thought which existed now as if it had been there since the creation. There was no feeling in his mind, nothing but the thought, and so the pressures of the body were once more notable. There was a weight on his chest over the heart, pains in his two arms, and a pain in his right cheek. He opened his eyes, and found that he had the spire gripped to him, and his right cheek was ground against a sharp edge near the point. The tiles of the floor were before him once more, each with two heraldic beasts, their clawed feet raised to strike, their snakey necks entwined. Somewhere, either over these tiles, or perhaps where the angel had been, or in the infinite dimensions of his head, there was a scene like a painting. It was Roger Mason, half-turned from the ladder, drawn by invisible ropes towards the woman crouched by the wall. It was Goody, half-turned, unblinking; feeling the ropes pull, shaking her head, Goody terrified and athirst, Goody and Roger, both in the tent that would expand with them wherever they might go. And so distinct that it might have been written across the painting, there was the thought. It was so terrible that it went beyond feeling, and left him inspecting it with a kind of stark detachment, while the edge of the spire burned into his cheek. It was so terrible, and so allaying to all other feeling, that he had to give it words as his eyes examined the linked creatures on the floor before him.

'She will keep him here.'

Then he got to his feet without looking at the light, and went slowly towards the crossways through a kind of crashing silence. He came to the trestle, where the model lay on its back, and jammed the spire into the square hole. He went away down the nave, and across to the deanery, his own place. Sometimes he examined his hands curiously, and nodded gravely. It was not till late that night that any feeling came back; and when it did, he flung himself on his knees again, and water ran out of his eyes. Then at last his angel came and warmed him so that he was somewhat comforted and the picture and the thought endurable. The angel stayed with him and he said before he fell asleep; I need you! Before today I didn't really know why. Forgive me!

And the angel warmed him.

But as if to keep him humble, Satan was permitted to torment him during the night by a meaningless and hopeless dream. It seemed to Jocelin that he lay on his back in his bed; and then he was lying on his back in the marshes, crucified, and his arms were the transepts with Pangall's kingdom nestled by his left side. People came to jeer and torment him, there was Rachel, there was Roger, there was Pangall, and they knew the church had no spire nor could have any. Only Satan himself, rising out of the west, clad in nothing but blazing hair stood over his nave and worked at the building, tormenting him so that he writhed on the marsh in the warm water, and cried out aloud. He woke in the darkness, full of loathing. So he took a discipline and lashed himself hard, seven times, hard across the back in his pride of the angel, one time for each devil. After that, he slept a dreamless sleep.

CHAPTER FOUR

From that time Jocelin became very busy. He rode out, gaitered and splashing through the mud to the country churches which were in his gift, examined his vicars, and preached to their haggard congregations. He preached in the churches of the city where he was archdeacon. In the Church of Saint Thomas, when he was high up, speaking from the pulpit in the triforium and half way down the nave — and the people stood below him, looking up, a half-moon of them — he found that he was talking about the spire urgently, softly striking his clenched fist on the stone desk. But the people moaned and beat their breasts, not because they understood him, but because he spoke so urgently; and because it was a time of rain, floods, death and starvation. That morning when he returned to the cathedral the rain was blown away by wind and at last he saw the whole building again. But now it was a sane, factual thing, so many feet long, broad, high, with neither grandeur nor majesty. Then he looked up into the cold sky; but it was shut. So he went to his room in the deanery and stared out of the little window at the building, for the confinement of the window sometimes gave what he saw from it a kind of extra definition and importance, like a picture in a frame. But the building was still a barn. Though he knew this was an illusion,

the cathedral seemed to have sunk, too. Outside the
gutter at the foot of the wall, the earth had swollen with
water and pushed up the coarse grass, so that the stone
seemed to dint the earth and the main impression was
not now one of God's glory, but of the weight of man's
building. And his vision of the spire seemed far away as
a dream remembered from childhood. If he thought of
Anselm, since the old man was part of childhood, the
question of confession hung, poised in his mind. But he
shook himself irritably and said to the air through
clenched teeth;

'I am about my Father's business.'

At this time, he ignored another letter from the Lady
Alison.

Nevertheless, the wind brought a change. It cleared
away the clouds and purged the cathedral of stink,
through the open doors. The floods began to go down,
leaving rot and ruin, but paths that could be walked on,
and flint roads where a wagon might pass. When he
walked towards the west front now, he saw that the gargoyles had respite and waited motionless with straining
mouths for what might come next. He would stand,
thinking with what accuracy and inspiration those giants
had built the place, because the gargoyles seemed cast
out of the stone, burst out of the stone like boils or
pimples, purging the body of sickness, ensuring by their
self-damnation, the purity of the whole. Now that
the rain had gone, he could see the moss and lichen of
green and black, so that some of the gargoyles seemed
diseased, as they yelled their soundless blasphemies and
derisions into the wind, yet made no more noise than
death in another country. The saints and martyrs, the
worthies and confessors, dried out imperturbably at
the west end, having indifferently endured the winter,

67

just as they now waited indifferently to endure the sun.

He began to feel that perhaps a little energy was coming back. When he thought of his tool, Roger Mason, with the women circling about him, he could say to himself — 'She is a good woman!' — and believe that was enough. For things were picking up. There was less coughing in chapter, and only one death; death of the ancient chancellor who had tottered through his last door; and since this was a proper death in slow time and with all the appropriate ceremonies, it was a matter for rejoicing rather than sorrow. Besides the new chancellor was young and diffident. It seemed in the twinkling of an eye that the time came when the curtains in the cloisters were taken down so that the boys of the songschool played in the open or tried to climb the great cedar. Suddenly, coming through the west door one morning, he saw that the cathedral was full of earthly life again. People had come to stare down into the hole at the crossways, or up at the hole in the vault. Now that the floods had gone back into the river and the sky was full of broken blue, the waters sank in the pit at the crossways so that when Roger Mason lowered a candle, it found no reflection of itself. The army became cheerful, whistling as it climbed the ladders among the scaffolding round the south east pillar, whistling into the corkscrew stair that led up to the triforium. As it returned with arms or hod or basket empty, it whistled or sung itself into view, and marched as indifferently as the effigies looked, through all the sternness of Lent. The army made a constant noise, however Jocelin complained to Roger Mason. There was a constant adzing going on in the shed outside the north transept, and a constant banging and thumping from the roof over the vault. But Lent was a time of girding for Jocelin who knew that soon he would be in battle; so in that preoccupation, he was helpless before the cheerful army as a girl herding too many geese. Helplessly he heard the songs; helplessly he saw Pangall aped through the crossways; helplessly, he saw Roger and Goody in the tent.

But still he said : 'I am about my Father's business!'

Then one morning when he entered the cathedral (Lift up your heads, O ye Gates) and stood by the pit where no smell was, he heard a change in the noises from the vaulting. He strained back his head on his neck, and a grain of sky hit him, smack, breathtaking, unbelievable, wonderful, blue. As the edges of his small window sometimes gave a depth and intensity to what he saw through it, so the roof round the tiny hole made this glimpse into a jewel. Up there, they were laying back the lead, rolling it back on the rafters. The blue widened and lengthened, joined earth to heaven, straight up there, where one day and soon, the geometric lines would leap into a picture of infinity. His head was back, his mouth open, his eyes screwed up and watering. He saw the busy shapes of men who did as they were told but did not know what they were doing; he saw an edge of white invade the blue, then pass; heard Rachel come clacking, but took no notice of what she said, how long she stayed, or where she went; stood with painful, disregarded neck, exhilarated like a child running through flowers, until the widening patch blurred and became a sparkling cascade. At last he eased his neck and came down into a confusion of light, honey-bars from the windows, phantom lights that swam through his head and wrestled with the sliding afterimage of the sky.

From that time, whenever the army worked in the

roof, the sky looked straight down at the open, waiting pit. Presently the gap was interrupted by a pattern of rafters; then these were taken away, piece by piece. The army hauled in a vast tarpaulin on a sledge and ropes slid down to it from the vault. The ropes went up again with the tarpaulin and some singing. When the men knocked off, the tarpaulin kept out the sky, though the rain sometimes drummed on it, a shower like choir feet, or a roar. Then the men would come back when the weather was fine, and reveal the sky again. Every day, the master builder would inspect the pit. Once, he went down it himself, but came up with muddy feet, and shaking his head. He would say nothing, but this did not matter since Rachel explained the transaction to any who would listen, and to some who would not.

Lent moved on towards Easter, and there were complaints that the noise from the roof reached into the Lady Chapel, so that Jocelin saw it was now necessary for the dean to climb, and see things for himself. So he climbed a corkscrew stair laboriously and carefully, and came out at last in the vaulting, where the pit was no more than a black dot, a hundred and twenty feet below. He was in a wide square with battlements all round; there was air and light. He picked his way among the mystifying wood and stone and leaned out to see; and the square of the cloister was below him, with the bulge of the cedar in the middle. The boys of the songschool were playing tag on the grass, or bent over checkers on the sill of the arcade. It seemed suddenly to Jocelin that now he loved everybody with ease and delight. He was filled with excitement. When he drew in his head — a raven missed it by inches — there was matter for more excitement. For he saw that he was standing on a single course of new stone that ran right round the square. A mason was spreading mortar thin as the white of an egg. So Jocelin clasped his hands, lifted up his head and included the boys and the dumb man and Roger Mason and Goody in one tremendous ejaculation: 'Rejoice, O daughters of Jerusalem!'

So it was Easter, particularly in the Lady Chapel where the event announced itself by changes in the altar frontal, which became unbleached linen. There was unbleached wax in the candles, there was the driving out of the congregation, and the grave waited for an angel to say He is arisen. But in the crossways, where the light had nothing but grisaille to contend against, Easter proclaimed itself in another manner, with noise and sun.

After that the courses rose quickly, until as Jocelin looked from his window he could see how white stone rose above the battlements. Presently the rising square grew scaffolding on its own account, with a ladder, two ladders. The beams from Ivo's forest nosed into the cathedral through the gap in the north west transept. Ropes came down for them and they went up, end on, like arrows, and men kept out of their way. Jocelin wanted to see what happened to them, but the master builder put him off. When at last he climbed again, he saw how Ivo's beams — or his father's beams — had formed a base on four sides for a flooring where there used to be a roof. But there was a square gap in the middle, so that a torrent of sky still fell down it. The stone course on all four sides began to progress irregularly. They left gaps in themselves, and Jocelin understood that they had reached the windows, fifty feet high, which would give the tower its light.

There were flowers in the Lady Chapel and pale faces filled out and the mouths of children were sweet with praise. So Ivo came, robed to be made a canon. Before

71

three Principal Persons he read from the great bible, or recited, it was difficult to know which since he read Our Father and Hail Mary; but the new chancellor declared that now Ivo could read well enough. So the ceremony of installation took place in qualified sunlight from the life of St Aldhelm worked in the little windows. Jocelin sat in his stall, with a sense of the tower rising. He waited for Ivo who performed with dignity enough. So finally Jocelin received him at the west end of the Lady Chapel, and took him by the warm hand. There was the asking and the accepting, the leading hand in hand, the temporary stall; and at last among the candles and the flowers, the kiss of peace.

After that Ivo went back to his hunting.

All this time the air and the earth dried; and then the dust came again. The carefully laid plans for dealing with it were tacitly laid aside, for Pangall and his sweepers had lost heart. What mud had been left in the nave and the aisles dried and drifted. More dust came down from the square shaft over the crossways. It lay here and there in modest drifts and dunes. Sunshafts were bright with it, monuments held it in little films and screes. The crusaders who lay in heraldic silence on slabs between the pillars of the nave were no longer flamboyant with heraldry, but wore filthy chainmail, or dungcoloured plate armour as if they had been struck down then and there in the press. On this side of the wood and canvas screen, the body of the church was secular as a stable or an empty tythe barn. For the purpose of the building seemed concentrated in the funnel over the crossways. The scaffolding climbed up inside, so that to look up from the crossways was like looking up a chimney where very methodical birds had been building. Ropes hung, platforms reduced the square of

72

sky, uprights seemed to draw together, and ladders slanted from level to level. All this was threaded continually by the army. The noisy cheerfulness of spring died away, to leave behind it a quiet concentration. In the body of the church they had been rowdy and casual. But now, lifted nearly two hundred feet into the air, their individual mysteries laid hands on them, so that the noises were for the most part, blows, chipping, rubbing, scraping. Sometimes, on his way to service or meditation in the Lady Chapel, Jocelin would pause and peer up, to watch a workman plod along a bouncing plank that lay across a corner in the dizzy air. Sometimes he would follow a single stone from Pangall's Kingdom, watch it go up stage by stage in a hod, or sway up the centre on a thread. He would watch the master builder climbing heavily and carefully from stage to stage, his T square under his arm, and a lead plummet hanging from his waist. He had an instrument for sighting, too. It was metal with a minute hole bored in it; and hour by hour he would sight along the walls, or from corner to corner. Every time he used the T square or the sighting thing, he would repeat the measurement the other way round, then drop the plumbline; so that at least two of the workmen would be idle. Jocelin would find that he was holding his own breath in exasperation at this idleness, till some necessary business of his position, a message brought by Father Anonymous perhaps, called him back to the wide world. At the first possible moment he would return to the crossways, and stand, squinting up and ejaculating, so that the young man who had now reached the third of the four head's of Dean Jocelin had a hard time of it.

Then, one day when he paused, he saw clusters of men in argument at the high top. He saw Roger Mason jollying and cajoling, losing his temper deliberately, or being reasonable, so that after hours wasted, the work limped on. After that, the master builder came down to ground level with Jehan and worked on the pavement. He brushed Jocelin aside testily. He set dishes of water on the pavement, chocking them up with slivers of wood, and sighted at them. He made a scratch on the stone of each of the four pillars of the crossways and drew a chalk mark over each scratch. From that time and at least twice a day, he was preoccupied with these marks. He would stand, for example, by a door in the south transept, and squint at each mark in turn, then look for their reflections in the dish of water. When the chalk dropped from a pillar, he marked it in again.

But Jocelin, passing happily through the crossways, laughed and shook his head at Roger. Sometimes he would call out to him.

'What! Still no faith, my son?'

The master builder never answered him and only once came near answering. It was after his angel had comforted Jocelin strongly, so that he felt if he were given the chance he could hold up the whole building on his own shoulders. When he came back to go down the nave (and there was Goody hurrying this way) he felt an urge to communicate his triumph and he cried out to Roger behind the dish of water.

'You see my son! I told you — They don't sink!'

Then Roger opened his mouth but said nothing for he saw Goody hurrying up the north aisle; and it was plain to Jocelin that the master builder forgot him when he saw her. So he went away down the nave, and his triumph felt a little tarnished at the edges.

Rachel was another drawback at this time. She would stand with Jocelin when he looked up, not looking up with him, but inevitably talking, chattering, interrupting, till once more the only defence was to ignore her. She had no head for heights, she said, and this was a great distress to her since so much of Roger's work was done in dangerous air. She waited, though, for Roger to go up and come down; and when they were at ground level they revolved round each other again, withdrawn from the rest of the world. Every time he saw this Jocelin thought to himself, with a horrid flinch, that they were more like brother and sister than man and wife, if it were not for the filthy, ludicrous thing he knew about them; he, dark, choleric, heavy but devious; she choleric, dark, strong and busy. And Pangall chipped away at a wall, or stood, leaning moodily on his broom, or limped away from the mocking army; and Goody Pangall passed through the crossways — but there were other ways she could get to her house — not looking up, with an effort that bent her neck; and Roger Mason, sighted at a chalk mark — Sometimes Jocelin surprised himself; or rather a dark corner of his mind surprised him, forcing his mouth to utter words that had no logical meaning, but seemed connected directly to triumph or uneasiness.

'There's much more to come.'

But then his logical mind would put the thing in perspective, and he would go, nodding towards the deanery, and wait for his angel, who gave comfort, but no advice.

Then it was June, and Jocelin came into the church with an aching head. The night before, contact with his angel had been particularly long and rewarding, and he thought at first timidly, then proudly, then timidly again in an infinite regression that exhausted his wits, that this might be because he had done well in forcing the tower up against all opposition, to the height of one window. Afterwards he realised that the angel had come to warn him; for the devil was allowed to assail him in a particularly loathsome way, so that to his waking mind in the morning, the last hour of sleep was vile with tempestuous visions. He came early as he could, to pray. It was daylight, so that he expected to find the army working. Yet the dusty barn was silent and deserted. When he got to the dry hole at the crossways and squinted up with a flash of fire through his head and an extra ache, he saw that all nests were bare of birds in the chimney, ropes swinging slowly in some draught, nothing else moving but a pink cloud which inched across the opening at the top till it closed the square with a glowing cover. He brought his eyes back down, and some wordless anxiety sent him hurrying to Pangall's Kingdom; but the cottage was silent, and the glasscutter's bench deserted. He came back to the church, hurried across the echoing crossways into the north transept, so that he could peer through the gap in the wall, to see if there were workmen about in the Close; and then he saw where the army was. They filled the shed where the beams had lain seasoning all winter. At the entrance were the women, silent and still. Further in, were men who stood on the beams that had not yet been shifted. Farthest in of all, was Roger Mason, his head and shoulders dark against the opened end of the shed. He was speaking, but not loudly enough to reach Jocelin; and besides, there was noise, and movement from the whole crowd of men.

As he peered round the rough edge of the hole in the wall, Jocelin nodded wisely and ruefully to himself, through the flashes of pain in his head.

'They want another penny a day.'

So he went away into the Lady Chapel, where the east windows were coming to life, and he prayed for the army. As if his prayer had called them, he heard them,

76

even before he was properly centred down, coming into the crossways with their noise and work. He turned to the business of the devil, with a twitch of disgust, and mourned the unruly member. But the noises from the crossways, and his own memories, were a hard thing to put aside. He found himself instead, kneeling, his chin on his wrist, looking at nothing, and thinking about things instead of praying about them. There's a crisis, he thought, and I must be strong for it.

Then he was jerked up out of himself. The dumb man stood by him, with no leather apron and no shaped stone in his hands, but humming with his empty mouth. He even laid a hand on Jocelin to pull him; and ran away again, into a commotion at the crossways.

I must go to them, thought Jocelin, as he watched the dumb man vanish through the flashes in his head.

He spoke aloud.

'I eat too little, and the Lenten Fasts exhausted me. Who am I that I should dare to mortify flesh necessary to the work?'

He heard shouting from the crossways, and the urgency of it got him on his feet. He hurried down the ambulatory and stood, blinking in the light of the crossways. The sunlight made haloes where his eyes looked out of his aching head, but he frowned at them with a fierce effort of will and they subsided. He could not tell at first what the trouble was, because Rachel came circling and babbling and it cost him some more will to shut her out. All the men of the army were in the crossways, the whole crowd of them. The women, except Rachel, were grouped in the north transept. Yet in the first few seconds of his entry he saw how more people joined those already there, whispered a little, then were still and tense as the others. It was as if all the players were present at an interlude, standing still, and waiting for the drum to sound. There was Goody Pangall, Pangall with his broom, Jehan, the dumb man, Roger Mason; it was as if they were clockfigures, frozen in attitudes of mechanical activity and waiting for the hour to strike. They were an irregular circle, and the centre of this circle was the open pit. On this side — and sick and fretful as Jocelin was, he recognised the cleverness of it — a sheet of metal had been set up on a trestle so that the sun was trapped and hurled straight down the pit. Jehan and the master builder crouched on the other side, looking down.

Jocelin went quickly to the pit, with Rachel clacking by him; but as he reached it, the master builder lifted his head.

'Everybody get further off — go on! Right into the transepts!'

Jocelin opened his mouth to speak; but Roger whispered fiercely at Rachel.

'You — get out of the light! Right out of the church!'

Rachel went. Roger Mason put his head to the edge of the hole again. Jocelin knelt by him.

'What is it, my son? Tell me!'

Roger Mason went on staring down the hole.

'Look at the bottom. Keep still, and watch.'

Jocelin leaned forward on his hands, and a weight of hot water seemed to run from his neck into the back of his head, so that he had trouble in not crying out. He shut his eyes tightly and waited for the flashes of sickness and pain to go out of them. By him, he heard Roger whisper.

'Look right at the bottom.'

He opened his eyes again, and the reflected sunlight in the pit was easy to them. It was peaceful, secluded. He could see the different kinds of soil all the way down.

First there was stone, six inches of it, the slabs on which they knelt; then, as it were hanging from this lip, the sides became fragmented stone held together with accretions of lime. Beneath that again was a foot or two of furry things that might be the crushed and frayed ends of brushwood. Beneath that was dark earth, stuck everywhere with pebbles; and the bottom was a darker patch, with more pebbles. There seemed little enough to look at, but the quiet light from the metal sheet was restful; and no one made any noise.

Then, as Jocelin looked, he saw a pebble drop with two clods of earth; and immediately a patch perhaps a yard square fell out of the side below him and struck the bottom with a soft thud. The pebbles that fell with it lay shining dully in the reflected light, and settled themselves in their new bed. But as he watched them and waited for them to settle, the hair rose on the nape of his neck; for they never settled completely. He saw one stir, as with a sudden restlessness; and then he saw that they were all moving more or less, with a slow stirring, like the stirring of grubs. The earth was moving under the grubs, urging them this way and that, like porridge coming to the boil in a pot; and the grubs were made to crawl by it, as dust will crawl on the head of a tapped drum.

Jocelin jerked out his hand and made a defensive sign at the bottom of the pit. He glanced at Roger Mason, who was staring at the grubs, lips tight round his teeth, a yellow pallor shining through his skin which was not all reflection.

'What is it, Roger? What is it?'

Some form of life; that which ought not to be seen or touched, the darkness under the earth, turning, seething, coming to the boil.

'What is it? Tell me!'

But the master builder still strained down, eyes wide open.

Doomsday coming up; or the roof of hell down there. Perhaps the damned stirring, or the noseless men turning over and thrusting up; or the living, pagan earth, unbound at last and waking, Dia Mater. Jocelin found one hand coming up to his mouth; and all at once he was racked with spasms, and making the same sign over and over again.

There came a sharp scream from by the south west pillar. Goody Pangall stood there, her basket still rolling at her feet. From below the steps that led up to the wooden screen cutting off the choir, there came an imperious smack; and flicking or flinching that way, Jocelin saw bits of stone skittering out like pieces of smashed ice on the ice of a pond. One triangular piece the size of his palm slid to the edge of the pit and dropped in. And with the piece of stone, came something else; the high ringing of unbearable, unbelievable tension. It came from nowhere in particular, could not be placed, but sounded equally at the centre of things and at the periphery; it was needles in either ear. Another stone smacked down so that a leaping fragment clanged on the metal sheet.

All at once there was a tumult of human noises, shouts and curses and screams. There was movement too, which as it began, became at once violent and uncontrolled. There were many ways out of the crossways and no two people seemed to have the same idea about how to go. As he got to his feet and backed hastily away from the pit, Jocelin saw hands and faces, feet, hair, cloth and leather — saw them momentarily without taking them in. The metal screen went down with a crash. He was jerked against a pillar and a mouth — but whose mouth? — screamed near him.

'The earth's creeping!'

He put his hands to fend off and somewhere the master builder was shouting.

'Still!'

And marvellously all the noise died away so there was nothing left but the high, mad ringing of tension. As it died, the master builder shouted again.

'Still! "Still!" I said! Get stone, any stone — fill the pit!'

Then the noises broke out once more, but this time in a kind of chant.

'Fill the pit! Fill the pit! Fill the pit!'

Jocelin crouched against the pillar as the crowd swirled and shredded away. Now I know what I must do, he thought, this is what I am for. So as the edge of the crowd came back — two hands bore a head of Dean Jocelin and hurled it into the pit — he crept past the pillar and into the ambulatory. He went, not into the Lady Chapel, but into the choir, and knelt in a stall as nearly under the key of the arch as he could get. The singing of the stones pierced him, and he fought it with jaws and fists clenched. His will began to burn fiercely and he thrust it into the four pillars, tamped it in with the pain of his neck and his head and his back, welcomed in some obscurity of feeling the wheels and flashes of light, and let them hurt his open eyes as much as they would. His fists were before him on the stall but he never noticed them. He felt confusedly and mutinously; It is a kind of prayer! So he knelt, stiff, painful and enduring; and all the time, the singing of the stones operated on the inside of his head. At last, when he understood nothing else at all, he knew that the whole weight of the building was resting on his back. He passed, in this frozen attitude, through a point of no time and no sight. It was only when he was puzzled by the two shapes in front of him, that he realised he had come back from somewhere; and looking round the flashes of light — but now they were glossier and swam rather than jerked — he saw the shapes were his two fists, still ground into the wood where he had put them. Then he knew something was missing, and his mouth strained open in sudden fright, till he realised that the stones were no longer singing; and this was perhaps because they had done whatever work it was they had come to do in his head. So he looked past his fists; and there was Roger Mason, standing, smiling a little, and waiting.

'Reverend Father.'

Suddenly Jocelin was back in the world; but not entirely. Too much had altered, too much been rearranged. He moistened his lips, allowed his fists to unclench; yet there was that within him which he could not unclench.

'Well, Roger, my son?'

Roger Mason smiled even more broadly.

'I've been watching you, and waiting.'

(And can you see how my will burns, Bullet Head? I fought him, and he didn't win.)

'I'm always here for you when you need me.'

'You?'

The master builder put his hands to the back of his head and moved it sideways as if he were freeing it from something. That's what it is, thought Jocelin. It's freed him. He thinks it's freed him. He can't see. He doesn't know. For the moment there's a kind of ease in him.

The master builder let his hands down and nodded thoughtfully, as if he conceded a point.

'Right, Father. I've never denied your interest — even your enthusiasm. You couldn't know of course. But things have settled themselves, haven't they? And I'm glad, in a way. No. Not in a way; in every way. Things have come to a point.'

'What point?'

Roger Mason laughed easily, in the dim choir, like a man at peace.

'It stands to reason. Now we must stop building.'

Jocelin smiled with his lips. He saw Roger from a long way off, and small. Now, he thought. We shall see.

'Explain yourself then.'

The master builder examined the palms of his hands, knocked dust off them.

'You know as well as I do, Reverend Father. We've gone as high as we can.'

He grinned at Jocelin.

'After all, you have one light completed, one window. You can have a pinnacle at each corner, and four heads of Dean Jocelin — we shall have to cut them again, by the way — one above each window. We'll lead in a roof and you can put a weathercock in the middle. Do more; and the earth'll creep again. You were right, you see. It's incredible even for that generation; but there aren't any foundations. None at all worth having. Just mud.'

Careful of the weight on his back and the suggestion of his angel's return, Jocelin sat upright in his stall and folded his hands in his lap

'What would satisfy you, Roger? I mean, by the rules of your art, how could you make the spire safe?'

'I couldn't. Or put it this way, there's nothing I can do. If you had all the time and money in the world, let alone the art and skill — well then; we could take down the cathedral stone by stone. We could dig a pit a hundred yards each way, and say, forty feet deep. Then we could fill it with rubble. But the water would get there first of course. How many men with how many buckets? And imagine the nave, standing all that time on the lip of a cliff of mud! You see, Father?'

Jocelin looked away for a moment at the altar through the fire of his head. This is what it is, he thought, this is what it is to offer oneself and have the offer accepted.

'You're a man for a very little dare.'

'I dare as much as most.'

'That's still very little. Where's your faith?'

'Faith or no faith, Father, we've come to the end. That's all there is to it.'

And this is how a will feels when it is linked to a Will without limit or end.

'There's building work to be had at last, Roger. Malmesbury, isn't it?'

The master builder looked at him expressionlessly.

'If you say so.'

'I know so and so do you. You'd find safe wintering there, and work for your army, you think.'

'Men must live.'

There was a sudden burst of noise from the crossways that fanned some feeling into irritation. Jocelin shut his eyes against it and spoke angrily.

'What was that?'

'It's my men. They're waiting.'

'For our decision.'

'The earth made it for us!'

The master builder's deep breathing came close to the shut eyes.

'Finish now, Father, while there's still time.'

'While there's other work for the army.'

Now the master builder's voice was angry too.

'All right then. Have it your own way if you like!'

He felt the breathing go away, and put out his hand quickly.

'Wait a moment. Wait!'

He put his clasped hands on the desk and bowed his forehead gently on them. He thought to himself; presently my whole body will be on fire, my pulse a blinding one. But this is what I am for.

'Roger? Are you there?'

'Well?'

'I'll tell you a thing. What's closer than brother and brother, mother and child? What's closer than hand and mouth, closer than the thought to the mind? It's vision, Roger. I don't expect you to understand that —'

'But of course I understand!'

Jocelin lifted his face and smiled suddenly.

'You do, do you?'

'But there comes a point when vision's no more than a child's playing let's pretend.'

'Ah!'

He shook his head, slowly and carefully; and the lights swam.

'Then you don't understand at all. Not at all.'

Roger Mason moved over the smooth tiles and stood looking down.

'Reverend Father. I — admire you. But the solid earth argues against us.'

'Closer than the solid earth to the foot.'

Roger put a hand on either hip, as if he had made up his mind. His voice was louder.

'Listen. You can say what you like. I've made the decision for us.'

'You're breaking it to me, then.'

'I understand in a way what it means to you. That's why I'm prepared to explain. There are other things, you see. They trapped me.'

'The tent.'

'What tent?'

'Never mind.'

'I might have been caught — but now the building's impossible, I can go away, go right away, forget, however much it costs me.'

'Break the web.'

'It's only gossamer, after all. Who ever would have thought it!'

Carefully, his eye on the open trap, Jocelin nodded at the animal.

'Only gossamer.'

'And there's another thing. What's his priesthood to a priest? There's a thing you have a right to know about, Father. You could call it Builder's Honour.'

'With more work for the army at Malmesbury.'

'I'm trying to tell you!'

'So you can keep this honour and the army too. Things aren't as easy as that. They cost more than that, Roger.'

'Well then. Forgive me.'

Goody Pangall and Rachel began to circle through the fire in his head. All the faces of the Chapter — I had a vision. I would protect her if I could — protect all of them. But we are each responsible for our own salvation.

'There's no one but you who can build it. That's what they said. Notable Roger Mason.'

'There's no one at all.'

And from the crossways; a shout of anger, then laughter.

'Who knows, Roger? Perhaps a braver man —'

Stubborn silence.

'You're asking me to release you from a sealed contract. I can't do it.'

Roger's words were a mumble.

'All right then. Whatever happens, I've decided.'

Escape from the web, from cowardice and little dares.

'Take time, my son.'

He heard more shouting from the crossways, and the master builder's feet begin to move away over the tiles. Once more he held out his hand.

'Wait.'

He heard the man stop and turn. Where have I come to, he thought dizzily. What am I about to do? But what else can I do?

'Well, Father?'

Jocelin answered him fretfully, hands over his eyes.

'Wait a moment. Wait!'

It was not that he needed time; for the decision had made itself. He felt behind his eyes a kind of sick apprehension, not because the spire was in danger; but because the spire was not in danger — never more strongly ordained and planted, more inevitably to be built. And therefore he knew what he must do.

He began to tremble from head to foot, as the stones must have trembled when they began to sing. Then, like the singing, the trembling passed away, left him still and cold.

'I wrote to Malmesbury, Roger. To the abbot. I knew what was in his mind. I let it be known how long we shall need you here. He will look elsewhere.'

He heard quick steps towards him in the choir.

'*You* — *!*'

He lifted his head and opened his eyes carefully. There was not much light left in the choir, and now, what there was, seemed all run into dazzles and haloes that lay round every object. They lay round the master builder, who clutched with both hands the edge of the desk. His hands had clamped on it and moved as if they would twist it apart. Jocelin blinked at the haloes and spoke quietly, because he did not like the echo of the words in his head.

'My son. When such a work is ordained, it is put into the mind of a, of a man. That's a terrible thing. I'm only learning now, how terrible it is. It's a refiner's fire. The man knows a little perhaps of the purpose, but nothing of the cost — *why* can't they keep quiet out there? *Why* don't they stand quietly and wait? No. You and I were chosen to do this thing together. It's a great glory. I see now it'll destroy us of course. What are we, after all? Only I tell you this, Roger, with the whole strength of my soul. The thing can be built and will be built, in the very teeth of Satan. You'll build it because nobody else can. They laugh at me, I think; and they'll probably laugh at you. Let them laugh. It's for them, and their children. But only you and I, my son, my friend, when we've done tormenting ourselves and each other, will know what stones and beams and lead and mortar went into it. Do you understand?'

The master builder was staring down at him. He no longer wrestled with the wood but held on as if it were a plank in a whirling sea.

'Father, Father — for the love of God, let me go!'

I do what I must do. He will never be the same again, not with me. He will never be the same man again. I've won, he's mine, my prisoner for this duty. At any moment now the lock will shut on him.

Whisper.

'*Make me go!*'

Click.

Silence, long silence.

The master builder let go of the wood, backed slowly away through the haloes and the turbulent noises beyond the screen. His voice was hoarse.

'You just don't know what'll come out of our going on!'

Backing away, eyes wide; pause in the door of the choir.

'You just don't know!'

Gone.

Silence from the crossways. He thought to himself; it's not the stones singing. It's inside my head. But then the silence was slashed by a fierce yell, and he heard Roger Mason shouting. I must go, he thought, I must go, but not to him. I must go to my bed. If I can get there.

He laid hold of the stall and pulled himself upright. He thought; it's his business not mine. Let him settle it, my slave for the work. Carefully he went across the choir and into the ambulatory. At the steps he paused and lay back against stone, his head back, eyes shut, trying to gather strength. I must pass among them, he thought, for all their shouting; and he tottered down the steps.

He was struck by a gust of laughter; but not for him. The noises were as confused as the lights that swirled in his head. The place was a mass of brown tunics, leather jerkins, blue tunics, clothbound legs, wallets of leather, beards and teeth. The mass moved and swirled and its noise defiled the holy air. He glimpsed the hole that still gaped in the pavement; and saw between the legs that it was not entirely plugged yet. He knew this was some nightmare; since things happened and stuck in the eye as if seen by flashes of lightening. He saw men who tormented Pangall, having him at the broom's end. In an apocalyptic glimpse of seeing, he caught how a man danced forward to Pangall, the model of the spire projecting obscenely from between his legs — then the swirl and the noise and the animal bodies hurled Jocelin against stone, so that he could not see, but only heard how Pangall broke — He heard the long wolfhowl of the man's flight down the south aisle, heard the rising, the hunting noise of the pack that raced after him. He understood, the breath almost out of his body, how the dumb man knelt over him, with a weight of brown bodies falling, turning, pressing down on his back. And as he lay, waiting for the shuddering arms to spring apart and the weight to crush them both, he knew that something else he had seen was printed on his eye for ever. Whenever there should be darkness and no thought, the picture would come back. It had been — it was — it would always be Goody Pangall on the surround of the south west pillar where the tide of the army had washed her. Her hair had come out into the light. It hung down; on this side splayed over her breast in a tattered cloud of red; on that, in a tangled plait which doubled on itself, and draggled with green ribbon half-undone. Her hands clutched the pillar behind her, hiphigh, and her belly shone about the slit of navel through the handtorn gap in her dress. Her head was turned this way, and always, till the end of time, he would know what she was looking at. From the moment of the tent there could be nothing else for her to look at — nowhere else she could turn that white, contracted mouth, but towards Roger on this side of the pit, his arms spread from his side in anguish and appeal, in acknowledgement of consent and defeat.

Then the dumb man's arms leapt apart.

CHAPTER FIVE

⁂

When he came to himself in his room, the singing began again, though he had forgotten where it came from. Therefore the singing was a great anxiety to him, an urgency that made him turn his head from side to side, the more so, because he was locked in his head with only a few things. These few things sorted themselves endlessly but never arrived at any order. There was a kind of watershed in circumstances, and he knew this was connected with an interview he had had somewhere, perhaps in the choir, with Roger Mason. There was a fall and tangle of red hair on green cloth, with the stone of the pillar behind it. This worried him endlessly for however much he tried he could not recreate the peaceful woman behind the hair, the woman as she was, coming into the west end peacefully, smiling, pausing to cross herself at his blessing. It was as if the red hair, sprung so unexpectedly from the decent covering of the wimple, had wounded all that time before, or erased it, or put a new thing in the way of the succession of days. So he would try to recreate the woman and the secure time, but find himself looking at the red hair instead. But always there was the high singing, and these other things were hung on it.

Father Anselm came stiffly to confess him; but all he could remember was that he intended to change his confessor, so Father Anselm went away. After that, Jocelin began to send urgent messages; for he thought the army must have stopped working. But Father Anonymous brought back a strange answer.

'They're working quietly and well. There's no trouble at all.'

So Jocelin saw that the work was still in no human hands.

Then he asked about Roger.

'He's wandering here and there. He's looking for something, they say. But no one knows what.'

'And the woman?'

'She goes with him as always.'

'I mean the other one. The one with red hair. Pangall's wife.'

'She is seldom to be seen.'

It is shame, thought Jocelin. What else can it be? She has broken out of the tent, and those men saw her half naked, her hair fallen.

But Father Anonymous was speaking again.

'As for her man himself, Pangall; he's run away.'

Then Jocelin's head preached Father Anonymous a sermon on the cost of building materials. It was a sermon which had the unusual property of returning to its beginning, however far you wandered like a planet. At some point in the sermon, the sick head fell into a deep and relieving sleep. When it woke up it knew where it was and what was going on. Moreover in sleep it had been given something new, a kind of reinforcement, as if it had gone to ground for repairs rather than recovery. This was a blazing certainty, that made the old one seem no stronger than the stubbornness of a child. I must get up, he thought; and with the thought, he was out, swaying and laughing. He found Father Anonymous hurrying towards him, and clapped the little man on the shoulders with both hands.

'No, Father Anonymous! Let me go! There's work to do!'

There was the necessity in these words of two notes of a high laugh. They followed logically. Then he was down the stairs and out into the September sun and he waded laboriously through the air at ground level, swaying from side to side as though he were wading through tall corn. He stopped breathlessly by the west door and pulled himself together, then went inside with all the painful happiness of the new certainty blazing in his head.

Immediately he caught sight of the pillars at the crossways, he remembered that he knew where the singing note had come from; and when he remembered, the note stopped, so that the inside of his head was as silent as the stones. He stood there for some time, enjoying the silence, and with the silence came a little awareness of himself as human, more or less. He understood that all small things had been put on one side for him, business, prayer, confession, so that now there was a kind of necessary marriage; Jocelin, and the spire. He saw the master builder talking to one of the men by the scaffolding, so he waded towards them, panting a little. He was glad to sit on the plinth round the north west pillar and lean his back against it. The workman went away, climbing deftly towards the brightness in the tower; and Jocelin called out to the master builder.

'You see I am back, Roger!'

Again, each word built up a kind of pressure which had to issue at the end in two notes of a high laugh. He knew he was laughing when he did it, and knew laughter was unsuitable, but was too late to take any effective measure. The laugh came out and the tower sucked it up. That was bad, he thought. I mustn't do that again. He looked back at Roger Mason, but the master builder was following the workman, ascending methodically, heavily, ladder after ladder. Jocelin craned back, and watched him climb where the square chimney with its geometrical birds was soaring to heaven height. He saw how sheer the white stone rose, with sheer lights, where even now the glaziers were wiring in the squares of grisaille. It was a new place in the sky, and sunlight was slashing it through, so that as Roger Mason climbed like a bear, the sunrays wheeled round him. Then Jocelin understood that it was partly the power of his own head that was thrusting the master builder up, up, and would continue to do so, until by some contrivance of his art, he swung the great cross into place, four hundred feet in the air at the spire's top. But the lightness of the chimney with its cap of cloud dazzled him, so that he bent his head, rubbing the water out of his eyes, then blinked at the floor by his feet. It was almost hidden. Chips of stone and wood, shavings, splinters, stone dust, dirt, a plank, and something that might have been the broken end of a besom — all the mess had been pushed back roughly against the pillars, shoved out of the way, to leave a clear space in the centre where the paving was replaced over the pit. He was vexed at this and the testy words were already there in his head — *Where is Pangall?* — when he remembered she was deserted. So he rubbed his forehead and told himself that the man would be quite incapable of staying away from a building which meant the world to him. He will come back, he thought, even if it means waiting till the army's gone. And I must do something about his Goody, he thought, then looked round him, expecting for no reason whatsoever to see her somewhere. But the church was empty of everything but dust, sunlight, high noises from the chimney, and the muffled sound of the choir in the lady chapel. I must see that she lacks for nothing, he thought; and then he could not remember why. Among the rubbish at the bottom of the pillar he saw there was a twig lying across his shoe, with a rotting berry that clung obscenely to the leather. He scuffed his foot irritably; and as now so often seemed to happen, the berry and the twig could not be forgotten, but set off a whole train of memories and worries and associations which were altogether random. He found himself thinking of the ship that was built of timber so unseasoned, a twig in her hold put out one green leaf. He had an instant vision of the spire warping and branching and sprouting; and the terror of that had him on his feet. I must learn about wood, he thought, and see that every inch of it is seasoned; and then he remembered that the spire was not begun nor the tower completed to the top; so he sat down again and blinked up.

The hole through the vault into the chimney was smaller, because some of the beams that would make a flooring for the vast apartment of the lower stage were already in place. But there was still a wide space left in the middle for the lifting of stone and wood. Yet the beams seemed to confine and define the busy world up there next to the sky, so that it was correspondingly brighter among the wielded sunrays, the moving bears, the scaffolding, ropes and near-vertical ladders. There was even a hut hanging in a corner at the top, like a swallow's nest. As he looked, he saw the master builder back out of the hut and go to do something with his sighting instrument. I never knew how much it would mean, he thought. I tried to draw a few simple lines on the sky; and now my will has to support a whole world up there, before I can do it. And the twig may have come from the scaffolding, which perhaps does not need to be seasoned, and in any case, will be taken down when they have finished.

He heard the familiar tap and scrape; looked across; and there was the young man seated by the south west pillar, a new piece of stone in his lap. Jocelin got up and waded across. The young man stood up quickly and put the stone by him, then stood there, smiling and nodding and clapping his hands softly.

Jocelin blessed him.

'My son. I owe my life to you, it seems.'

He felt his high laugh coming with the words and succeeded in making a giggle of it. The young man spread his arms wide and shrugged.

'Were you injured yourself?'

The young man laughed soundlessly, and touched his nose, which indeed, was thicker on the bridge and shinier there. Then he stretched out his right arm, bent it, grinning and fingering the biceps. With a sudden rush of love, Jocelin threw his arms round the young man and embraced him, clinging as to a pillar or a tree.

'My son, my son!'

The young man glowed, and hummed, and patted his back timidly.

'I shall do something for you, my son.'

The young man was quiet in his arms, still patting, pat, pat, pat. He is my son, he thought, and she is my daughter. But the red hair fell and blinded him, so that he shut his eyes and groaned. Then he discovered how tired he was and his bed drew him. That night his angel came again; and after that, the devil tormented him a little.

96

Day by day getting a little strength, he watched the summer prolong itself as if in recompense for the storms and floods of spring. The leaves turned at last, and lay tinder dry. The coarse grass round the cathedral broke under his feet; was brown and brittle as the leaves left in a besom; and now the gargoyles, taking part in some infinite complexity of punishment, gaped as though they sought water in the dry air. There was no point of rest for them. They were in hell, could expect no less, that was all there was to it. In this dry air, his will, his blazing will, was shut down to a steady glow, that illuminated and supported the new building and nothing else. So the young man chipped and the builders climbed, Rachel circled round Roger; and Goody Pangall was to be glimpsed far off at the end of an aisle, wimpled head down, a woman about her work, the red hair hidden. If she seemed about to come near, she circled him quickly, looking away and hurrying on, head down as if he were an unlucky corner, or a ghost, or the grave of a suicide. But he knew that she was only ashamed with the shame of a deserted woman; and her shame squeezed his heart. But my will has other business than to help, he thought. I have so much will, it puts all other business by. I am like a flower that is bearing fruit. There is a preoccupation about the flower as the fruit swells and the petals wither; a preoccupation about the whole plant, leaves dropping, everything dying but the swelling fruit. That's how it must be. My will is in the pillars and the high wall. I offered myself; and I am learning.

Sometimes he would find Rachel circling in the crossways, talking to anyone who passed, then pausing to peer up at her bear climbing in the tower; voluble Rachel who would abandon everything else at sight of the Dean, to come to him. Then one day he found her easy to deal with. He ignored her completely, detaching himself from the sound of her at his elbow. When she circled to get in front of him and question him, he did not hear her question but only felt it as an interrogation mark left in the air. He stood there, looking down at her. He noticed that she seemed older, and strained, but the change did not interest him much. Even when he saw how she had taken to painting her face, he felt nothing but a distaste that emerged as a twitch of his body, concealing the high giggle. After that, he decided he was bored with looking at her, and he looked through her instead without saying anything, so he never saw the astonishment under the red paint.

As the days passed he found this indifference very useful. It enabled him to treat the chancellor with courtesy when he came to the deanery, without allowing himself to notice what he came for. In some cases — the precentor was one — this useful technique led to a look which he decided afterwards was downright consternation. Then in the foggy days of Autumn, when a vast tarpaulin shut out the sky at the growing point of the tower, he discovered he could always stop these people at any moment he wanted to. He would merely say — and this was after Father Anonymous pointed out that he never read any correspondence unless it was connected with the spire — would say : 'I must get back to the building.'

Despite the tarpaulin, the fog got into the church; but still it could not interfere with his will. Nor did it interfere with the young man who still chiselled and scraped. Surely, thought Jocelin, as he examined the second of the four heads that had filled the pit, surely they are leaner than they should be ? And isn't the mouth too wide open ? Can eyes ever be as wide as that ? But he said

98

nothing of all this; for he loved his son in God as he loved his daughter in God; and the young man had not only preserved his life, and therefore the will that held up the pillars, but looked at him frankly, like a good dog, which Goody, if she was caught near enough, never did.

So she irked him, and her red hair irked him, and he felt nothing about her but compassion for her shame, and a strange disquiet. By the beginning of December the four heads were finished and vanished up the chimney with the young man, to where the four upper lights were waiting for them. On the morning when he watched them go up, Rachel was circling again, chattering. Since he was free for the time being of the young man, the thought of Goody came on him with full force, in Pangall's desertion. Why have I neglected her? She needs me! And as if the thought of her had created her for him, there she was, hurrying up the north aisle, looking up — and now swerving aside, going on past the crossways into the ambulatory, faster, faster.

'My child —'

He thought; I must do it for her sake, though it interrupts my concentration. And he went quickly to the south exit of the ambulatory; and there she came, hurrying again, and now ducking aside.

'My child!'

Laughing but half vexed, he moved across, arms spread, so that she could not pass. She stood under the wall, sideways and shrinking. Her hair was decently hidden, her face turned away so that he could see little but the long hollow of one cheek.

'My child, I have been meaning —'

Meaning what? What have I to tell her? What am I to ask her?

But she was speaking up to him, pleading.

'Let me go, Father. *Please* let me go!'

'He'll come back.'

'Please!'

'And meanwhile — all these years — My child, you are very dear to me.'

With a sudden shock, he saw how white her lips were, white and drawn in against her teeth. He could see too, how wide and staring, wide, dark eyes could be, as if the eyelids had been drawn back, like the lips. The basket jerked up against her breast, and he could only just hear what she whispered.

'Not you *too*!'

Then she was gone, gasping and sobbing, and slipping past him, to race down the dark ambulatory, so that her heavy cloak flapped in the air, and beneath her skirt he glimpsed her ankles and feet.

He put his hands on either side of his head and spoke angrily out of the depths of his confusion and incomprehension.

'What's all this?'

Then he shook himself, for he felt her cling, and this was bad for the work. I must put aside all small things, he thought. If they are part of the cost, why so be it. And if I cannot help, what is the point of all this brooding? I have too great a work on hand. Work! Work!

He had a thought so brilliant he knew it had been put into his mind. It was an illumination. I must climb away from all this confusion! And with the thought came the high, fretful laugh again. I shall take this burning will of mine up the tower. He looked down at his gown and saw that it was not designed for climbing; but he bent and pulled the back hem through his legs and twisted it up into his girdle. A workman coming down, stood aside on

100

the first staging and knuckled his forehead. Suddenly everything was easier in Jocelin's head. There was sunlight at last, flashing round him. He climbed again and again; came to the dark and unwalled platform of the triforium and ducked into a stairway lighted by nothing but arrow slits, as though the building might have to be defended by archers. He came out of the stair and the new beams above the vaulting lay before him. He climbed again, up wide ladders by the flash and glitter of the lower tower windows.

'Of course,' he cried, 'Of course!'

He felt his heart hitting his ribs and he rested a while to slow it and get his breath. He perched on the edge of a staging like a raven on the edge of a cliff. The men climbing up and down, looked at him curiously but said nothing. He hutched to the very edge and let his legs hang over. He clutched an upright with both hands, leaned round it and looked down.

The shafts, wall and windows of the tower drew together below him, and seemed everywhere only just thick enough to bear their own weight. Everything was clean and new. The eighty foot lights of the windows, two in each of the four sides, the platforms and uprights, the ladders and newly adzed beams, were clear with present light. He felt the same appalled delight as a small boy feels when first he climbs too high in a forbidden tree. He felt his head swim, and encouraged his own dizziness and caught breath by squinting straight down — down, down, hole after hole depth after depth to the distant world of the crossways. The pavement was as dim as the bottom of the pit had been, discoloured by depth and the dullness of ground level. Then the dizziness passed to leave thought and delight behind it.

'Of course!'

So a bird must feel, free in a world of branches and the liberty of wings. So grey we must seem, so reduced to our heads and shoulders, so shackled, crawling over the earth, and as he thought that, he saw Rachel crawl across the pavement from one side to the other as though she were something stirred out of the earth itself. He felt free of her and he turned back to the mounting ladders. He got up and he clambered on, heedless of the white impropriety of his thighs. More than two hundred feet up in the air, they became proper. He went from level to level, looking up always at the verge where the men worked themselves towards the sky. The noises of building became loud about him again. He stopped for his breath by the swallows' nest and found it was a room, large as his own, and hanging in one corner with an unglassed gap looking into the shaft of the tower for light. The master builder was sighting by it from this stone here to that one across the tower. Jocelin stood radiantly by him on the four planks, and shouted out of the necessity of height and exhilaration.

'You see, my son! The pillars don't sink!'

The master builder answered sourly, still peering at his instrument.

'Who knows what anything does? Perhaps each pillar stands on its own foundation.'

'I told you, Roger. They float!'

The master builder shook his shoulders irritably.

'I can hear you well enough.'

'Roger!'

He put out a hand, but Roger Mason pulled away as though his body were tender to the touch. He swung round on the plank nearest the white wall, and clutched his sighting instrument to his chest.

'I told you years ago, Father — and now!'

'How can you speak so, Roger, with a, a miracle all about you? Can't you feel it? Can't you get strength from it, learn from it, see how it changes everything?'

They were silent, looking at each other in the noises of scraped stone. Roger Mason examined him slowly, from the toes of his shoes, along the shins, the white thighs, up past the body to the face. They stood eye to eye, and the master builder smiled grimly.

'It's changed things all right.'

He turned away, opened the door of the swallows' nest; then jerked round and shouted furiously.

'And can't you see what you've done?'

Then he was gone, slamming the door so that the nest shook round him.

Jocelin looked at the walls.

'I know! I know! Indeed I know!'

He was swept by a sudden gust of joy that took him laughing to the ladder; and by the time he had climbed it, he had forgotten Roger Mason and the pavement below him.

For this was the growing point, the top. Three planks led round it on every side and the builders were working there. It was a place of little speech. The men bent outward and worked at knee height on a wall that varied in level by the height of a stone before them. Here, it was only one stone high above the planking but with mortar already spread thinly while the workmen manoeuvred the next stone; there — and this was the same in all four walls — no stone appeared above the plank at all, but only wood, shaped to the key of an arch. The stones of the arch had drawn together partway along each curve, but left a gap where the keystone would be; and he knew that each arch contained the lights below, drew them together, swept up and over, so that all their transparencies would seem part of one thing, a single deed. By each wooden form, lay a stone head, shouting silently and exulting in the height of heaven and the brightness. The young man knelt by one and did something to the face with his graver — looked up, and laughed silently as the head, across the reeling gap. Jocelin found himself laughing back, genuinely with pleasure for the new things and the miracle. A thought came into his head with the laughter and he shouted it across to the young man careless of dignity.

'Up here we are free of all the confusion!'

And the young man laughed back, a good dog; then bent to his work again.

Also there was a new noise. This was not speech or chipping or banging. It was constant, not deep or thick enough to be a purr, and not sharp enough to be the stones singing. He listened carefully and discovered that it was the touch of the wind up here on stone. He knelt down, then sat, his arm laid across the stone of the wall and listened to the wind. For a while he was at peace and his thoughts had their way with his head, popping in and out; and he was content to let them do so.

This world of stuff, was a new thing. Down there, the model had been so slim and so delicate, the butt so easily to be held in two hands, the lights such a gentle tracery on every side; but up here, the paper thinness of the walls became a cliff of stone, and the needlelike members of the interior, beams on which two men could walk side by side. Suddenly he became aware of the weight suspended so miraculously and even in his content, the world seemed to turn over. I must be kinder to Roger, he thought. This weight which meant nothing to me was in his head all the time. Also he has no faith.

Then to right the swimming world, he concentrated

on the model again, the model down there in the dimness of the nave. But when he concentrated, unlooked-for things came with the spire, things put aside, from the time when the earth crept and the stones began to sing. He found himself once more holding his breath and listening. He saw for an instant between a blue tunic and a brown one, Pangall at the broom's end, one of the army dancing towards him, the spire projecting obscenely between his legs. He saw a fall of red hair. And then he found himself gripping the stone, eyes shut, mouth open, while the ribs tightened round his breath. The confusion was in his head again. He said dizzily to himself; it's the cost! What else should I have expected? And I can't pray for them since my whole life has become one prayer of will, fused, built in.

Have mercy. Or teach me.

But there was no answer. Only the touch of wind on stone.

He opened his eyes and found that he was looking away from the tower and out into the world : and it had changed in nature. It had bent itself into a sort of bowl, detailed here, sweeping up beyond that to a blue rim. In astonishment and delight, he laid hold of the stone and heaved himself into kneeling. This is what it must mean to be a bird, he thought — and as if in illustration, a raven slipped past his face, slanting on the wind with a harsh expostulation at the people lifted so boldly into its kingdom. Beyond the raven — and now Jocelin let go the stone and stood up so that he could see over the bending workmen — the valleys of the three rivers that met by the cathedral close opened themselves up. The rivers glittered towards the tower; and you could see that all those places which had been separate to feet and only joined by an act of reason, were indeed part of a whole. To the north east he could pick out three separate mills, three separate cascades at different levels, all joined by leagues of water that snaked towards the cathedral. The river did indeed run down hill. He saw the white stones of the new bridge at Stilbury, saw the very nuns, or two of them at least, in their garth, though they were enclosed, and this distant inspection a breaking of the wall. Remembering this, he concentrated on the new bridge, screwed up his eyes and saw a straggling line of packmules, asses, draughthorses, pedlars and beggars on foot, country people with their loads of vegetables drifting towards the stalls at the north end of the bridge. It was market day in Stilbury then, though not here in the City, a fact known before to reason, but now all swept under one eye and seen to be so. His joy beat at him like wings. I would like the spire to be a thousand feet high, he thought, and then I should be able to oversee the whole county; and he wondered at himself, remembering whose spire it would be. And as if in answer, he thought he felt his angel at his back, warming him in the wind. Now it is true, without any doubt; up here, among the tapping and clinking and scraping, here, moving towards the clouds, I am cheerful as a child that sings. I didn't know I could still be as happy! So he stood on the planks in the wind and let the happiness calm all the confusions in his head. He examined the strips and patches of cultivation, the rounded downlands that rose to a wooded and notched edge. They were soft and warm and smooth as a young body.

He got down on his knees, hard, eyes shut, crossing himself and praying. I bring my essential wickedness even here into thy air. For the world is not like that. The earth is a huddle of noseless men grinning upward, there

106

are gallows everywhere, the blood of childbirth never ceases to flow, nor sweat in the furrow, the brothels are down there and drunk men lie in the gutter. There is no good thing in all this circle but the great house, the ark, the refuge, a ship to contain all these people and now fitted with a mast. Forgive me.

He opened his eyes and stood up, looking for his happiness to see where it had gone, looked up into the air where the rest of the tower and the spire would be, an unthinkable height. A great bird floated up there on spread wings, and he said aloud, remembering Saint John : 'It is an eagle.'

But the young man who was working at a mouth, looked up too, then smiled and shook his head. Jocelin went over to him along the planks, bent and tugged his curly hair.

'Well. As far as I am concerned it is an eagle.'

But the young man was at work again.

At the nearer edge of the downs, there were knobs and lumps appearing, as if bushes were growing by magic. As he watched, they pushed up, and became men. Behind them were more knobs which became horses, asses in foal with panniers, a whole procession of travellers with burdens. They came straight over the nearer ridge from the one so bluely outlined behind it. They were moving straight down the hill towards his eye, towards the tower, the cathedral, the city. They had not gone by the west, circling down by Cold Harbour to make their way slanting along the deep trench that generations of hooves had cut. They were saving time, if not labour. In a flash of vision he saw how other feet would cut their track arrowstraight towards the city, understood how the tower was laying a hand on the whole landscape, altering it, dominating it, enforcing a pattern that reached wherever the tower could be seen, by sheer force of its being there. He swung round the horizon and saw how true his vision was. There were new tracks, people in parties, making their way sturdily between bushes and through heather. The countryside was shrugging itself obediently into a new shape. Presently, with this great finger sticking up, the City would lie like the hub at the centre of a predestined wheel. New Street, New Inn, New Wharf, New Bridge; and now new roads to bring in new people.

I thought it would be simple. I thought the spire would complete a stone bible, be the apocalypse in stone. I never guessed in my folly that there would be a new lesson at every level, and a new power. Nor could I have been told. I had to build in faith, against advice. That's the only way. But when you build like this, men blunt like a poor chisel or fly off like the head of an axe. I was too taken up with my vision to consider this; and the vision was enough.

He looked down at the tiny rectangle of Pangall's kingdom, where now there were far fewer piles of stone; saw the small square of the cloisters. He could even see the white counters that the songschool boys had left on the sill of the arcade from playing their game of checkers. He looked round at the houses, ranged along the limits of the close. Over the red roof ridges, back-yards were open to him, spotted with cows and pigs. He watched an old man go heavily into a privy, and secure between his walls, leave the door wide open. Three houses away was a woman, a small patch of white and a large patch of brown, and she was preparing to go from house to house. She had two wooden pails and the yoke lay near against the wall. Screwing up his eyes, he could make out that the pails contained milk; and he smiled grimly to himself as he watched her top up each pail with water. He watched her lift the pails, vanish under the roof ridge and appear again in the street, then cross the road to avoid the drunk man who lay in the gutter beating time feebly with his arm while a dog lifted its leg over him.

'The slug.'

He swung round, startled. But Roger Mason was not looking at the drunk man. He was looking away, down to the south east and the invisible sea.

'The louse.'

Seven glittering reaches away, there was a huddle of houses by the river.

'What can you see, Roger?'

'Look at him the thief! He'll be in the Three Tuns. He'll leave his barge alongside with our good stone in it, while he swills himself all night and all tomorrow. For all he cares we can wait and whistle!'

'My son —'

The master builder bawled at him.

'What's it to me? Or you? You won, didn't you?'

Then there was stillness. Daze, like after a blow. Faces lifted. No scraping or tapping.

'Gently Roger. Gently.'

'Gently! I —'

Roger Mason put his hands up to his face. He spoke harshly from behind them.

'You men. Get back to your work.'

Presently the tapping began again. But Roger Mason lowered his hands without looking at Jocelin. He went away, saying no more, and made his bear's way down the ladders, paw after paw.

Jocelin watched him go down, and a new knowledge came into his head. I dread to go down there, he thought.

Here is my place. But it must be done, since no man can live his life with eagles. So he forced himself, down the ladders, past the swallows' nest, down on to staging after staging, down the corkscrew stair to the dim world, to the dull, factual pavement at the bottom of the pit. He had a message for the master builder but Rachel flitted between them so that he could not entirely detach himself from her babble — looking better for the exercise my lord she wished oh how she wished she could follow Roger to the top of his craft but heights were a real purgatory to her — painted face jerking in spate, body jerking — had to stay down in this mess at the crossways it was a real crime the way Pangall deserted his duty, so like a man, well not all men, not like some she could mention, to go off into the blue without so much as a message and leaving his Goody with child at last on top of it, poor soul, sweet soul, such a *dear* person and now to be left —

A great anger swamped Jocelin, rage at the drunk man in the gutter and the sot in the Three Tuns. He cried out to Roger's averted face.

'My son! You must use my authority. Send a man on a good horse to the Three Tuns. Let him take a whip with him, and let him use it as necessary!'

Then he was walking away down the nave from the mess and the babble, walking away, and tears streamed down his cheeks. Oh the lessons I have learned, he thought, the height and power and cost!

By the west door he had got himself together again. He turned and spoke thickly to the High Altar.

'Thou hast heard my prayers, O Lord: and these are tears of joy because Thou hast remembered Thy handmaiden.'

CHAPTER SIX

⟨∾∾⟩

When he returned to the spire, the hosannaing
heads were built in at the top of each window.
He leaned over the growing edge of the wall,
and saw them there from above, each with hair blown
back, each with a nose projecting like a beak. They
shouted at the tracks which feet were cutting in the
downland, they ignored the birds that perched and muted
whitely on them. As he looked down the well of the
tower, he could see how the vaulting had been rebuilt, so
that only a circular hole was left through which the eye
could find the dim pavement; pavement so dim as to
be almost invisible. But beams came up end on through
the hole to where the workmen received them. He took
part — or observed, shoved into a corner — in a sort of
insanity of creaking and banging and shouting as the
beams were laid at the top of the tower to form a floor
halfway up. For the tower was to rise another eighty
feet in another chamber, with more lights, more hosannaing heads, more platforms and ladders, so that the
mind winced to think of it; winced at any rate up here,
where solidity balanced in midair among the birds, held
its breath over a diminishing series of squares with a
round hole at the bottom which was nevertheless the
top.

And the work, as he knew, experienced in the con-

111

suming steadfastness of his will, the work was blessed. There were astonishing days in December, when the church never knew the sun, when the nave was like a cavern. On those days, it was hard to do anything in the dark church but endure one's will, knowing that in the end all would be well, though the weight of the lower chamber and the weight of the second chamber now growing, were a strain to be experienced right inside the head. On those days he would climb eagerly, like a child that seeks comfort from its mother. Only he did not care to think of a mother. If he did, Goody with her hidden red hair would stab his mind and prick tears out of his eyes.

On such a day, he passed through the close from the deanery to the west door, hardly able to see his feet for fog; and though the nave was clear of it, like a sort of bubble, it was near enough pitch dark. He climbed, and came out of the corkscrew stair on to the beams, and in a blinding dazzle. For up here, the sun was shining; and even those rays that pierced the chamber were faint against another light that blazed upwards, lit lead and glass and stone, lit the underside of the beam roof, so that the very adze marks were visible. Then when he climbed through this dazzle to the upper chamber, up the ladders and levels to where men were working with blue hands and came at last on the ragged top — then he was pained and blinded indeed, and had to press his palms to his eyes. For there was downland visible all round but nothing else. The fog lay in a dazzling, burning patch over the valley and the city, with nothing but the spire or the tower at least, piercing it. Then he was strangely comforted, and for a time, almost at peace.

But there were other days when the fog drowned even the tower. Then the work would slow down or stop, and he would be shut in at ground level with the cost of everything. The army would work as at the bottom of the sea, in sheds and arbours. They shaped wood. In a shed near the wound in the north transept, there were octagons of beams, each smaller than the one below it. They grew, and were piled taller than a man. The carpenters marked them curiously, part by part, then took them to pieces again, while the master builder brooded on a lattice model of small stick that made a shape like a dunce's cap. Few people approached him, for he had become unpopular with his men. He was too sullen, too curt, too apt to burst into raging flames of temper, then fling off by himself, with Rachel, strained, painted Rachel, clacking and circling round him. And since Jocelin had come to feel a great compassion for this slave of the work, it was hard to see him climb so slowly, so dourly, hard to see him standing, staring up or down, using his sighting instrument with the same care; or standing in the crossways, listening.

For there was often something to listen to. Late in December the stones began to sing again. They did not sing all the time; and in the Lady Chapel there were whole weeks together when the choir could sing unhindered. But then men would be aware of some vague discomfort, and trying to define it, would decide that the air was too dry or too cold; only to find at last that there was a needle in each ear, and that breath had a tendency to hold itself for no reason whatever. Then the needles would become audible, so that breath let itself out in a long expiration, to be replaced by exasperation and fear. Even the people of the city, and travellers from distant parts, would come to the west door and stand there listening for the threat and the marvel of the singing pillars; but they never came to the crossways as they had done in the early days. When the workmen heard the singing they would pause and look at each other, then bend to their work again. There was not much laughter among them. Only Jocelin, impaled on his will, would find a cheerful answer to the needles in each ear.

'It will pass.'

Nevertheless, as the winter moved towards spring, and the crocuses towards the surface of the earth, and the tower towards the sky, the stones sang more frequently.

It was at this time that Jocelin discovered something else about the master builder. He had watched him anxiously, assessing him as a tool for building, had counted his steps on the ladders, had waited for the moment when he would need to be resharpened or have the wedge driven more firmly into his haft; but he had come out of all that examination with no more than a knowledge of how Roger Mason looked, and moved. Then one day, looking down at the hole over the pavement, he watched him coming up the tower; and understood to his astonishment that the master builder feared heights as much as Rachel did. He feared them but he endured them. He lived with them, they were part of his craft; but he never enjoyed them as Jocelin did, never seemed to know the breathcatching exultation of a quivering plank up here, where you could no longer hear the stones singing, a quivering, bouncing plank over a sheer drop. So in his new knowledge, Jocelin watched him compassionately as he came up; saw him climb methodically, slowly, never casual as some of the workmen were, saw him looking always at the nearest thing to hand; saw the shaft to the dim pavement beyond the hole, understood why he trod for preference an inch or two nearer the wall than the centre of the ladder. There

was a little rain blowing, which clung to Jocelin's hair,
but he stood freely at the top in the push of the wind
and waited for Roger who was reduced to head and
shoulders with the net visibly round him.

'Why are you afraid, my son?'

The master builder stood before him, breathing
deeply. He grasped the parapet with an arm.

'They're singing again.'

'What of it? They've sung and stopped before.'

He looked up into the thin rain.

'Do you know, Roger, I've been thinking. That cross
up there — the cross that will be up there.'

'I know it.'

'Won't it be taller than a man? Yet on the model it's
the sort of trinket a child might wear round his neck.'

The master builder shut his eyes and gritted his teeth.
He groaned.

'What is it, Roger? What do you want to tell me?'

The master builder looked at him against the sky and
spoke huskily.

'Have mercy.'

'Not again!'

'Reverend Father —'

'Well?'

'This is enough.'

Jocelin continued to smile; but his smile stiffened. The
master builder flung out his free hand.

'They are overcome by the splendour of what we —
of what you —'

He turned away, leaned both elbows on the parapet,
put his face between his hands so that his voice was
muffled.

'I said, have mercy.'

'There's no one but you.'

Then the master builder was silent for a while, face in hands. He spoke at last without lifting it.

'I'll try to tell you about my mystery. The stones are singing. I don't know why, but I can guess. That's the trouble, you see. I always guess. When you come down to it, I know nothing. Or not as you —'

He looked up sideways at Jocelin.

'Or not as you know when you speak to a congregation. You see?'

'I see well enough.'

'I tell you, we guess. We judge that this or that is strong enough; but we can never tell until the full strain comes on it whether we were right or wrong. And then the wind, this wind that does nothing but stir the hair round your head —'

He stared angrily at Jocelin.

'Have you a machine to measure the weight of the wind, Father? Give me that, and I'll tell you what will stand and what won't.'

'But still the pillars aren't sinking. I told you.'

'They've begun to sing.'

'Have you never known a building sing before?'

'Never. We're surrounded by new things. We guess; and go on building.'

He bent back his thick neck and stared into the sky.

'And now the spire; another hundred and fifty feet of it. Father — this is enough!'

The will spoke calmly out of Jocelin's head. He heard it.

'I understand you, my son. It's the little dare all over again. Shall I tell you where we've come? Think of the mayfly that lives for no more than one day. That raven over there may have some knowledge of yesterday and the day before. The raven knows what the sunrise is like.

Perhaps he knows there'll be another one. But the mayfly doesn't. There's never a mayfly who knows what it's like to be one! And that's where we've come! Oh no, Roger, I'm not going to preach you a sermon on the dreadful brevity of this life. You know, as well as I do, that it's an unendurable length, that none the less must be endured. But we've come to something different, because we were chosen, both of us. We're mayfly. We can't tell what it'll be like up there from foot to foot; but we must live from the morning to the evening every minute with a new thing.'

Roger was watching him closely, tongue licking at his lips.

'No. I don't know what you mean. But I know how much the spire will weigh, and I don't know how strong it'll be. Look down, Father — right over the parapet, all the way down, past the lights, the buttresses, all the way down to the cedar top in the cloister.'

'I see it.'

'Let your eye crawl down like an insect, foot by foot. You think these walls are strong because they're stone; but I know better. We've nothing but a skin of glass and stone stretched between four stone rods, one at each corner. D'you understand that? The stone is no stronger than the glass between the verticals because every inch of the way I have to save weight, bartering strength for weight or weight for strength, guessing how much, how far, how little, how near, until my very heart stops when I think of it. Look down, Father. Don't look at me — look down! See how the columns at each corner are tacked together. I've clamped the stones together but still I can't make them stronger than stone. Stone snaps, crumbles, tears. Yet even now, when the pillars sing, perhaps this much may stand. I can give you a roof over

117

it, and perhaps a weather vane that men will see for miles.'

Jocelin was suddenly very still, very wary.

'Go on, my son.'

'The sheer impossibility of the spire! You need to be thrust this high Father, to understand it, don't you see? It'll be a stone skin with stone members. Inside there'll be a series of those octagons, each a little smaller than the one below it. But the wind, Father! I should have to pin those octagons together, and hang them from the capstone so that they hold the skin down by their weight. Weight, weight, weight, weight! All added to this; all boring down on the columns, on the skin of the wall, down on the singing pillars —'

Now his hand was on Jocelin's sleeve.

'And even that isn't the end of it. However I contrive, the spire won't thrust perpendicularly. It'll thrust at the tops of these four columns and it'll thrust — *out*! I could put pinnacles on each to bear down — should have to — but there'd be a limit to the height I could make them, because of the weight. At what point should I have to give up the one for the other? Oh yes; we could put in the first octagon and the second and perhaps the third —' his hand clenched on Jocelin's arm '— but sooner or later there'd be a new noise in the building. Look down again, Father. Sooner or later there'd be a bang, a shudder, a roar. Those four columns would open apart like a flower, and everything else up here, stone, wood, iron, glass, men, would slide down into the church like the fall of a mountain.'

He was silent again for a moment. Then his voice came, no more than a whisper.

'I tell you — whatever else is uncertain in my mystery — this is certain. I know. I've seen a building fall.'

Jocelin's eyes were shut. Inside his head, a series of octagons, each made of oak beams a foot thick, had built themselves up and up. For a moment, as he stood with gritted teeth, he felt the solid stone under him move — swinging sideways and out. The dunce's cap a hundred and fifty feet tall began to rip down and tear and burst, sliding with dust and smoke and thunder, faster and faster, breaking and sheering with spark and flame and explosion, crashing down to strike the nave so that the paving stones danced like wood chips till the ruin buried them. So clear was this that he fell with the south west column that swung out over the cloister bent in the middle like a leg and destroyed the library like the blow of a flail. He opened his eyes, sick with falling through the air. He was clutching the parapet and the cloisters were moving below him.

'What must we do?'

'Stop building.'

The answer came pat; and even before his sickness had sunk away and the cloisters steadied, some deep centre of awareness understood how the master builder had led up to this answer.

'No, no, no, no.'

He was muttering and understanding and shaking his head. He understood the plea refused, the final resource, building talk, a mystery not displayed down there on the solid earth, but pondered on, brought up the tower in privacy, used at last like a lever on a fulcrum of vertigo; all so contrived as to bring the will within a single moment of defeat.

'No.'

At last the reply was assured. It was the reply of one blade to another, clash, slither, clash.

'Roger, I tell you the thing can be done.'

119

The master builder flung away furiously, stood in the south west corner with his back to Jocelin. He faced the rain and looked at nothing.

'Listen Roger.'

What can I tell him? I talked about mayfly but ten minutes later and I can't remember what. Let the will talk to him.

'You tried to frighten me as you might frighten a child with a ghost story. You thought it out carefully, didn't you? And yet you know you can't go. Can't go. Can't get away. And all that time, your curious, valuable mind was finding a way round the impossible. You found it too, because that's what you're for. You don't know if it's the right answer but it's the best one you've got. But you're frightened. The best part of you would like to try, but the rest snivels and whimpers.'

He stood next to the broad back and spoke into the rain and the nothingness.

'Now I'll tell you what no one else knows. They think I'm mad perhaps; but what does that matter? They'll know about it one day when I — but you shall hear it now, as man to man, on this very stump of a tower, up here with no one else to listen. My son. The building is a diagram of prayer; and our spire will be a diagram of the highest prayer of all. God revealed it to me in a vision, his unprofitable servant. He chose me. He chooses you, to fill the diagram with glass and iron and stone, since the children of men require a thing to look at. D'you think you can escape? You're not in my net — oh yes, Roger, I understand a number of things, how you are drawn, and twisted, and tormented — but it isn't my net. It's His. We can neither of us avoid this work. And there's another thing. I've begun to see how we can't understand it either, since each new foot reveals a new effect, a new purpose. It's senseless, you think. It frightens us, and it's unreasonable. But then — since when did God ask the chosen ones to be reasonable? They call this Jocelin's Folly, don't they?'

'I've heard it called so.'

'The net isn't mine, Roger, and the folly isn't mine. It's God's Folly. Even in the old days he never asked men to do what was reasonable. Men can do that for themselves. They can buy and sell, heal and govern. But then out of some deep place comes the command to do what makes no sense at all — to build a ship on dry land; to sit among the dunghills; to marry a whore; to set their son on the altar of sacrifice. Then, if men have faith, a new thing comes.'

He was silent for a while, in the prickling rain, looking at Roger Mason's back. It was my voice that spoke the words, he thought. No. Not my voice. Voice of the devouring Will, my master.

'Roger?'

'Well?'

'You'll build it to the top. You think those are your own hands, but they aren't. You think it's your own mind that's been working, nagging at the problem, and now sits in secret pride of having solved it. But it isn't. Anymore than my mind speaks the words that are using my voice.'

Then they were silent again; and he was aware of the third with them, the angel that stood in the cold and rain, warming him at his back.

At last the master builder spoke, toneless and resigned.

'Steel. Or perhaps steel. I can't tell. We can pass a great band of it round the whole tower up here and bind the stones together. I don't know. No one has ever used as much steel as that before. I still don't know. And it'll cost more money, much more.'

'I'll find it.'

He reached out, timidly almost, and touched the master builder's shoulder.

'Roger — He isn't needlessly cruel, you know. Why, to those who need it because they're weak, perhaps, he even sends a comforter to stand at their back! He warms them in the rain and the wind. And you're necessary. Think how the chisel must feel, ground, forced against the hard wood, hour after hour! But then it's oiled and wrapped in rag and put away. A good workman never uses a tool for something it can't do; never ignores it; takes care of it.'

He paused, thinking. I speak of myself, perhaps, as much as of him. It was joy once; but strangely, no longer joy. Only a longing for peace.

'And Roger — when you have done and it stands here for all to see — the net may break.'

The master builder muttered.

'I don't know what you mean.'

'But build quickly — quickly! Before you consent to the major evil and the net never break —'

The master builder swung round, head down and lowering.

'Keep your sermons to yourself!'

'— because you have all become precious to me — you and all the rest — and I begin to live by you.'

'What d'you mean?'

What did I mean, he thought. I meant something about Goody and Rachel — I must speak to her as I spoke to him, or as the Will spoke to him.

He nodded seriously at the master builder.

'I must go down now, Roger. There's something I have to do.'

So he began to climb down the ladders with his angel; and before he was out of sight, he heard Roger Mason speaking softly.

'I believe you're the devil. The devil himself.'

But he dropped below the voice and the pillars were singing again; and by the time he reached the pavement of the crossways, their singing had put his purpose out of his head.

Then the tower stopped growing for nearly a month, but broke instead into a grove of pinnacles, twelve of them, three at each corner, with a master pinnacle at the centre of each group. Roger Mason spent less time up there, leaving the workmen to Jehan, who used them cheerfully, and got a joke out of every stone. So Jocelin was forced to go about his proper business and try to catch up with it, though it still lay a long way ahead of him. But the master builder lived for the most part at ground level, talking with iron workers; and Rachel talked with him. They got away from Jocelin by this means; and since the top of the tower was so crowded, he only saw the work in craning glimpses. He watched, while two hundred and fifty feet up in the air, a soundless Jehan jollied the stonecutters into making slots in every projection so that a steel ribbon could run right round, and fit tidily against the stone. On the few occasions when he stood among the forest of pinnacles at the tower top, Jocelin saw how the long shed by the river was coming to life. It smoked. All day and half the night, the hammers rang there like a peal of untuned bells; and when darkness came, he could see the reflection of the fires in the river. Inside the shaft of the tower, two floors closed off all but the central well. As the pinnacles rose, workmen took away unnecessary scaffolding by the ton. They lugged the members from the walls and filled most of the holes with stone. What holes were left, the ravens and pigeons investigated with speculative interest. Soon there was little left but the ropes that hung down the central well, and one steep, wooden stair that zigzagged up round the wall. The only temporary structure left in the tower was the swallow's nest where the workmen kept their tools and the master builder his instruments; and since there would soon be ample room at the base of the spire itself, even the swallow's nest was under orders to go. What scaffolding remained was now grouped round the tower top like a head of unruly hair; or like a stork's nest above the fantasticated, eighty foot fall of the lights.

Then, one day, Jocelin came from a rowdy meeting in Chapter where the news of the extra expense had been received with an incredulity which changed to indignation. In the end, with a flash of seeing, he understood that he would have to affix his own private seal to these documents, which he did in the deanery without more discussion. But the strain of chapter brought back his high laugh; and his angel was at once a blessing and a great wearisomeness to him; and because his own will slackened he could not control the thoughts and images that floated through his mind, images of the spire, of red hair, of a wolf-howl, till he longed for the strange peace of the tower. He went out into the close and heard suddenly how there was no noise at all and the world held its breath, for the shed was silent. He went into the nave, and found a little noise there between the services because the great pillars sang — eeeeeeeeeeeee — as if the strain had become intolerable. He went slowly and quietly up the corkscrew stair towards the peace and happiness where the pinnacles had grouped themselves. He went silently as a ghost; and that was why half-way up the wooden stairs of the tower, he heard the moan. It stopped him on the stair, back bent under the angel, each foot on a different rung, and hands gripping. It was the moan of some trapped animal, a roedeer, perhaps, past the time of kicking in the snare and now become nothing but helpless misery. He glanced sideways towards the swallow's nest. There was a gap at the top for light; and the gap was interrupted by an upright with the bark still on it. There was something else besides bark. A hand was gripping the upright; and Jocelin who had seen that hand many times — touching stone or wood, levelling an instrument, clenched in anger, or lifted in despair — knew the red and brown of it as well as he knew the paleness of his own. But the very moment he saw it, and recognised the touches of dirty white at the knuckles, and before he had time to think whom it implied, so passionately gripping wood, another hand, smaller, whiter, softer slid over it and held it tight.

Open-mouthed, motionless, unblinking, he stayed there on the stair; and heard her voice, voice of the moan, pleading, ingenuous and sweet.

'But I didn't laugh — did I ?'

The tough fingers leapt from the upright, the two hands wrung into each, vanished; and then the more familiar voice laboured up as if from the very pit bottom in the grey pavement —

'Oh God!'

He backed swiftly away down the ladder, mouth still open. He stood on the beams over the vaulting, bent his head and clapped his hands over his ears. He swayed from side to side, and stared round him through the stone walls. He felt his way to the corkscrew stair and went stumbling down it; and there in the darkness before his unblinking eyes the memories came storming in — a green girl running in the close and slowing decorously for my Lord the Dean, my reverend father, the shy smile and the singing of the child's game, noticed, approved, and at last looked for, yes looked for, expected, cherished, a warmth round the heart, an unworldly delight, the arranged marriage with the lame man, the wimpled hair, the tent —

'Oh no, dear God no!'

The cost of building material.

He came out at last into the church under the singing pillars and Rachel appeared circling, then positively at a run so that he let out his high giggle. And Roger was not at the foundry or the woodstacks was he up the tower or in the stairs, he needed food, he was exhausted — all the way down the nave into the twilight of the close she followed him, gabbing and clacking. He turned by the west door to bless her from his pain to hers: and saw her there before him under a weight of confessors, martyrs, saints, her red, illegal dress not yet settled into folds round the stocky body, her hands up to her mouth, no more words, strained, hurt eyes, popping out of the ageing, painted face. So he left her, and knelt at last in his own place, mouth still open, eyes open still, and staring at nothing.

By the evening of the next day, the swallow's nest was gone.

CHAPTER SEVEN

꧁ꡳ꧂

So he went to pray; but prayer had changed also. He was bent into a little grey space, tense and appalled, and when he glanced up to where help had been, a fall of red, knotted hair blazed there so that he would cower away from it. He would say to himself: I must offer all this up! And then, wordlessly, without his volition, he would find that his mind was making itself into nothing but a question: to where? If he deliberately detached himself from the hair, he might have a few moments of comparative freedom; and then, as if someone or something had taken it and brought it dangling, the hair was back, hanging in front of him, brilliant and real; and she would be back, with her green ribbons and torn dress and the black patches of her eyes staring across. So he would get up and go anywhere. Sometimes he would say 'Work! Work! Work!' briskly and speak urgently to people of business; then remember they knew nothing of it. Once, standing lost in his private storm at the west end of the empty cathedral, he saw her cross the nave, heavily and clumsily with child; and he knew in himself a mixture of dear love and prurience, a wet-lipped fever to know how and where and when and what. For it was as if the words in the swallow's nest were tugging him out of security into a chaos, where the four of them performed in some unholy marriage. When he came to himself for a moment, out of the whirlwind he found he had cried out, for the long stone shed of the nave was still echoing, but he did not know what he had said.

I must go to her, he thought, I must save what can be saved; but even as he had the thought, he felt the prurience in him like a leprosy, and knew that if he were to find her alone there would be nothing for it but to ask, and pry, and demand, without knowing what he wanted. Then he was suddenly aware of himself, a tall, gaunt man, standing in his cassock at the west end, his eyes staring at the wooden screen and his hands clenched. So he climbed again in the deserted tower past the place where the swallow's nest had been, which stabbed him and took away his breath. He made himself look from the tower — out into the world where other people went about their incomprehensible business; and he saw that for many of them that business had come to a stop. The tower with its grove of pinnacles had claimed them. The ends of the streets that led to the close were never empty. Men and women stood there, at that distance their faces no more than a blur, and looked up. As some left, others would come to fill their place. It was a continual drift and supply; and he felt a great bitterness as he looked at them, and he spoke into the wind.

'What do you people know about it all?'

The head of the tower was still, and matter-of-fact about him. He looked it over, a stone forest lifted up round the place where the spire was to be. This is nothing like my model, he thought — nothing like my vision; but we do what we can. Perhaps it's a diagram of the folly they don't know about.

Then he shouted aloud.

'Work! Work! Work! Why aren't they here?'

So he went quickly down the tower to find the master
builder; and by the time he reached the pavement his
irritation had become a mad anger. But the master
builder was working. He had assembled the army in the
shed by the north transept and was talking to them
gruffly out of his mayfly life. When Jocelin heard him his
anger died away, and became a restless eagerness to get
the thing done with; for Roger Mason was giving each
man directions, whatever his craft was. So Jocelin understood that they were dealing with the matter of the steel
band; and with the thing in hand, he took his inability to
pray back with him to the deanery, where his angel and
the devil visited him, and the unholy marriage stormed,
and he waited for the dawn. Sure enough, the great bell
in the detached belltower rang out of time, and all the
ways to the cathedral were noisy with talk and the sound
of feet. He went to see; but Roger Mason drove him
away from the tower itself with an authority that surprised and shook them both. So he walked and circled
like Rachel in the close; and then he went back to his
room, remembering what he had to do. He wrote a long
letter to the abbess of Stilbury, setting out certain facts
— but not all of them — and asking that on conditions,
a poor, fallen woman should be taken in. After that he
went to the nave, looked at the pillars and found himself
thinking that perhaps they felt as he did; but that at least
they could not feel this extra thing, this dreadful heaviness round the heart which was a purely human prero-
gative. Yet there was nothing to be seen of the work, so
he went to the long shed which was empty except for
the octagons and the master carpenter. The octagons
seemed heavy enough to defeat the highest wind; or so
the master carpenter said, as he swung his maul to strike
the sixth one apart, and there was in his voice something

which led Jocelin to enquire further; but the master carpenter would say no more.

Now the sun was well up and the shadows sliding back across the close to the high walls that had cast them. There was a new shadow among them, of the tower; and as it slid down away from the chancellor's house, Jocelin saw a kind of quivering indecisiveness about the end of it. So he hurried across the close almost to where the city people were grouped and waiting. When he turned on his heel and looked up, he saw that smoke was rising at the tower top. Wherever he went, circling and pausing, and whenever he stopped to look on that day, he saw how the smoke rose, never thickening but never ceasing, so that the sky trembled. When the shadows of the cathedral had crept out in the other direction the smoke still rose; and as darkness came, he could see a glow round the head of the tower — hear occasionally the voices of other men who lounged or slept or ate or drank by their buckets of water on the leaden acres of the roof. So he went to sleep; but was called out of his bed by a strange peal which came from the tower, the same tuneless peal that used to come from the shed by the river. He pulled on his cloak and went out into the close again through groups of laughing and chattering city people. Streams of sparks were falling from the head of the tower. They shot out of the glow at the top and they were not extinguished by the time the roof hid them. Once there was a scream from the tower, shouts and commotion, and for a while no more sparks fell. But before the watchers could decide what had happened, the sparks had begun to cascade down again; and presently a man came staggering through the door in the north transept, his arm wrapped in oilsoaked sacking. He paid no attention to Jocelin's questions, but went off towards

New Street, moaning and cursing. But there were plenty of people about to look after him if they chose to. It seemed to Jocelin that the whole city was awake, in the streets or the close, or behind open casements; and all looking up. Through the bland night, the tower glowed and sparked and smoked diminishingly among the stars. Then, an hour before dawn, the peal of tuneless bells rang no longer. Instead of sparks there came jets of steam shooting up, colourless as the unsunned stones and seeming a continuation of them. As day dawned, even the steam diminished. The airy furnaces, dribbling charcoal and water, crept down the fields of glass to where parties on the roof seized them and took them in. As the day brightened towards sunrise, Jocelin went forward, aching with hunger and sleeplessness to greet the men as they came down from the tower. But they ignored him. They came, swaying, staggering, with open eyes that looked through him at their distant beds; and their feet took them away. So he stood waiting for Roger Mason, in a sheer sickness of sleep. But Roger Mason never came. At last he went timidly into the crossways and climbed; and by the time he was out of the corkscrew stair he had forgotten everything but the physical being of the tower. For in that sunrise, with the beginning of a wind, the whole tower was talking, groaning, creaking, protesting, and every now and then uttering a bang! to stop the heart. But he reminded himself whose building this was, mastered the chattering of his teeth, and climbed up, past the corner where the swallow's nest had been, up the slanting stairs till he came out on the wooden roof among the forest of stone. There was a mess of charcoal and water. When he gripped the parapet and looked down, he saw the whole world staring up, in a blur of white faces — and

131

there was the band of steel, a foot wide and two inches thick, studded with blue rivets. Everywhere it lay close against the stone that was scarred and broken. But the band was alive and talking. It cried, wangle-angle-bangle-clang! it mouthed, and in the pauses of the mouthing, settled to a steady ringing.

He let himself down and knelt, staring between two battlements. I am here, he thought. This is what it's about. This is my place. I can't work wood or steel or stone; but this is what I am for.

So he crouched down to pray; but before he could pray, slumped sideways against the base of a pinnacle, he fell asleep, and his angel came, unseen with six wings and stood to warm his back.

He was awakened by the wind in his hair, awakened slowly out of dreams that slid away from him and left him alone with the wind. He opened his eyes; and in sudden vertigo knew that he was looking down at the cloisters, almost vertically down, two hundred and fifty feet. He shut his eyes again, screwing them up tight, and looking inward for the quiet place of dreams. But they had gone for good, and he knew this was another day inescapably, to be endured as the pillars were enduring. I've been faithful, he thought. We've come this far: and that idea was so comfortable that he lay in it for a while, then opened his eyes but thought no longer, while the wind pulled his hair round his cap and drew the last tear of sleep from his eyes.

Nevertheless, something was different, and he was forced back into thought, by the need to decide what the difference was. It lay in, or came to him, through his body, through the touch of hipbone, or cheekbone against the pinnacle — and bang! went the steel band as if to confirm that he thought rightly; might therefore be

132

some new quality in the stone itself. It was so subtle a newness that only this solitude, this close contact of flesh against the newly cut surface could detect it. It was a newness in the stone; in the stone all down his right side. This stone — and his hand felt out over it — this stone. And now more — less? more? solid when he touched it. He had a moment of fantasy when the stone seemed soft as a pillow, and he thought to himself; I am still half asleep! But a raven slipped past the battlements with a descending squawk that was sane and daylight and matter-of-fact. He lay there, looking down blankly at the cloisters, where sandalled feet and the hem of a gown strolled leisurely past, beyond the foreshortened arches of the arcade.

The boys of the songschool had left their game on the sill of the arcade again. He could not see the squares of the board scratched in stone, but he could see the white, bone counters of the game that lay on it. He could see some of them; but only some, for the stone between the battlements cut off a corner of the board from his eye. There was a kind of childish security in looking at the game, the white counters, one, two, three, four, five —

His cheek was hard against the pinnacle and he knew he had not moved. But a sixth counter had appeared, had slid into view with another square of board under it. He knew he had not moved; but he knew that the tower had moved, gently, soundlessly up here, though down there the pillars might have cried — eeee — at the movement. Time after time, he watched the white counter slide into view, then disappear again; and he knew that the tower was swaying under him like a tall tree.

Slowly he turned his eyes away and looked at the charcoal and drying puddles. I mustn't scream, or run, he thought. That would be unworthy of the vision. He got up carefully, feeling his weight on both feet. He went step by step, carefully down the talking tower, down the steep ladders, down the corkscrew stairs to a deserted church. The pillars were singing again; and now he understood something about the rhythm of their singing. He made himself stand in the crossways and listen as if it were a penance. Perhaps for a minute they would be silent; but then — eeeeeeeeeee — in full voice, hold the note, and at last, with the same gradations retreat into silence.

He looked down at the replaced pavement. It was here the vision came to me, he thought, on these very stones. Here I threw myself down, and offered myself to the work, all those years ago. And I've been faithful. It's in Your hands.

Then slowly, without looking back, he went away.

But the day had not done with him.

When he reached the deanery there was a man on horseback with a letter. The man had ridden the five miles back from Stilbury; and when Jocelin saw how quickly a letter could go and come, the first thought he had was that Stilbury was too near. The second thought was a more confused one of how Stilbury was quite far enough. But he took the letter and broke the seal and read. Yes, Stilbury would accept the wretched woman but on terms other than his, terms which amounted to a good sized dowry. He went to his coffer and took out money. I know what they will say, he thought. First Jocelin's Folly; and now Jocelin's whore. But I don't mind what they say. I've lived with derision so long I no longer notice it. This also.

He crossed the close again and went up the nave under

the singing stones, then across the south transept towards Pangall's kingdom. He stood in the doorway, looking at the slumped cottage, and it squeezed his heart small. So he stood there feeling the tide of misery rise. He thought to himself. This is the worst! Do this and I shall have peace. It must be done, for my sake and his sake and for the sake of my poor daughter.

So he braced himself to go to the cottage; but before he could take a step, he was jerked and staggered. There was a scarlet flash by his right eye and Rachel Mason rushed down the yard to the cottage, flung the door open and darted inside. At once, there was a crash from the cottage, screaming and shouting, Rachel shouting words that blistered. The door bounced open and the master builder stumbled out, his hands to the blood of his head. An instant later Rachel came out behind him. She screamed her hoarse imprecations at him, she struck him about the head and shoulders with a broom and there was a whisp of red hair caught in her fingers that flipped and flinked as she swung the broom handle; and all the time she screamed and shouted and foamed and looked at nothing but her target with her bolting eyes. The two of them stumbled past Jocelin without paying any attention to him; and he heard how the noise of justice multiplied in the cathedral — and he heard that there were workmen about now, for they were laughing. He stood, looking this way and that for a moment. Then he hastened down the yard and stood, holding money, in the open door.

Goody Pangall was half kneeling before the dull fire, where the black pot still swung slowly in little circles on its chain. Her weight was on her right hip and hands, and her legs were bent up beneath her. The light through the door gleamed from her naked shoulders, and her head was dropped, in a cascade of red, torn hair. She was gasping and sobbing and there was a kind of surging in her whole body. His long shadow fell across her. She looked, saw, and screamed. He put out a hand to stop her, but suddenly she stopped herself, seemed to gather herself, squatting round on her hams, and looking inward. She jerked up her legs, jerked them up under her skirt. She grabbed her belly with both hands and screamed again; but this scream was not like the first. It was short and sharp, like the cruel blade of a knife. And then she screamed just so, again and again.

The money fell from his hands. He turned and ran shouting up the yard into the south transept.

'Get the women here quickly! For the love of God! Oh my dear soul! A midwife!'

The workmen at the crossways started to run round and argue and shout. Jocelin ran back into the yard where the knife was still stabbing. He fell on his knees, praying incoherently have mercy, have mercy, I didn't know it was to be this, not this oh anything only stop the stabbing, the unendurable — but feet were passing him, there were shoutings and more argument. He got up and ran to the door of the cottage, to help, to do something, anything, have mercy. The workmen were holding up white, thin legs in the air, there was a white belly jerking and screaming under them, and there was blood over the money on the floor so that the world spun. When he came to himself he had to take part in a hideous ceremony of baptism; and then the women came, and father Anselm with oil and the Host which he thrust into the white, collapsed face. So Jocelin went away along the yard from buttress to buttress, leaning and clinging to the stone, a reed shaken in the wind. He found his way to the choir and knelt to pray for her, but the hair and the blood blinded the eyes of his mind. It was when she saw me, he thought. I was the church in her mind, I was the accuser and she fled from me. Oh Lord preserve her and I'll give what you leave me of my life to bring her peace — only stop the noise and the blood, and the stones singing in my head. It was more than a year ago I saw them and the tent was round them and the tent expanded wherever they went, and I consented under your eye. More than a year ago I —

He knelt there, seeing nothing but the woman in her storm. Now and then he shook himself and groaned. Now and then he spoke words.

'I was a protected man. I never came up against beldame.'

Then he forgot his knees, his hunger, forgot everything in a tumult of glimpses that presented themselves to him as if they were connected, though they had neither order nor logic. There was the arranged marriage and the swallow's nest. There was hair and blood, and a lame man with a broom limping through the crossways. He made no sense of these things, but endured them with moanings and shudderings. Yet like a birth itself, words came, that seemed to fit the totality of his life, his sins, and his forced cruelty, and above all the dreadful glow of his dedicated will. They were words that the choir boys sang sometimes at Easter, quaint words; but now the only words that meant anything.

This have I done for my true love.

Late that evening, while he still crouched and shuddered, father Adam felt his way along the darkening stalls, and told him that Goody Pangall was dead.

CHAPTER EIGHT

‿‿✖‿‿

So they put her body away in the raw earth and he wandered without seeing much. He wandered without saying much to anyone but himself, or at least to some nameless and invisible attendant. He would find himself walking down the south aisle one fist clenched by his chest; and then he would remember that he had been saying something, over and over again. Even when he could remember as he sometimes did — or even when he heard himself in the middle of a word — it would be a word that made no sense. He would stand, looking round his nose, head up, fists clenched. He would make positive efforts to control himself and find out what was the matter with him. Then he would be aware of a feeling rising in him, coming up towards the chest like a level of dark water. Often, his angel stood at his back; and this exhausted him, for the angel was a great weight of glory to bear, and bent his spine. Moreover, after a visit by the angel — as if to keep him in his humility — Satan was given leave to torment him, seizing him by the loins, so that it became indeed an unruly member.

Then again, he would find himself repeating one word endlessly, no, no, no, no, no, perhaps, or well, well, well, well; and at each word he would be tapping gently on the prieudieu with the flat of his hand. This was always when the dark waters in his belly — and now invading, tightening his chest — had risen a little. He would stand, facing the wall, laying his hand flat on it, numberless times, and find he had been saying nothing, nothing, nothing, nothing. The spire was there too, sketched in his head with simple geometric lines, but mixed with other things. Sometimes he would turn his inward eye on the spire; and that would set him hurrying to the crossways, to watch and encourage, however feverishly.

As far as some people were concerned, his eye had acquired a new facility. (Pain did it, pain did it, pain did it.) He saw with dreadful clarity of vision how the master builder had gone back to Rachel; or more correctly, was now seen by everybody to be her property again. (She is a good woman. She is a good woman. She is a good woman. Tap, tap, tap.) The two of them no longer flashed a quarrel at each other. They kept together, but they no longer revolved round each other. Roger Mason would stand watching his work, shoulders slightly bent, concentrating on whatever was to hand, and sullen. She would stand behind him and slightly to one side, not watching the work, but him. And watching them both with his new eyes, he saw the iron collar round Roger Mason's neck, and could follow the slack chain back from it to her right hand. If Roger climbed, she would stand there below, the chain in her hand, waiting to lock it on again.

Then he would have a feverish thought.

'Now, if I told him to build a thousand feet high, he would do it. I've got what I wanted.'

(No, no, no, no, no, no, hand pressing and relaxing, pressing and relaxing on the edge of a tomb.)

Once, his feet took him without his volition into Pangall's kingdom, where the door of her slumped cottage stood ajar. (God, God, God, pulling and twisting and tearing at the high stalks of weed.) So he hurried his feet back into the church, and went widdershins to the Lady Chapel. His mouth said the accustomed words but he saw, no, no, no, no, no, the white body and irretrievable blood. Then he thought of Anselm, but knew he could not explain these things profitably to that noble, empty head. (I must change my confessor, I must change my confessor, I must change my confessor.) But before he had done thinking that, he had forgotten what he said, because she was back again, with her tormented body and the terrible christening.

Then he let out his breath, looked closely at the grain of the wood before him, and spoke aloud, but humbly.

'I'm not very intelligent.'

As if his angel had whispered to him, there was help at hand.

'Think of her as she was before!'

And immediately he thought gladly of the girl coming from market with her basket and clumsy gentleness; and this stood him up and hurried him away laughing, so that he almost missed the chancellor. So he had to stand, nodding and smiling while the man talked. But his mind had gone back five happy years to the arranged marriage and while he was remembering it the chancellor disappeared. (Such a suitable, such an inevitable marriage, both fathers faithful servants of the church with their hands in their proper station.)

But I didn't laugh — did I?

(No, no, no, no, no, no, no, hand pressing and pressing and pressing —)

Hurry into the crossways for the major work, the essential complex, the reason, the burden laid; and Rachel, older, not so voluble, looking him in the eye, daring him to think ill of her — but who could? In the guild of married women she is a heroine, yes indeed, I must believe it, since she laboured and got back her man. But the pillars were singing again, and he forgot her as he listened, understanding how the fear had come with the singing, and driven the diminished congregations from the Lady Chapel.

(They are the little ones, the little ones, little ones —)

So he spoke aloud again.

'There are the great ones; the builders!'

As if in answer to him, a man came swinging down from the work. He carried his tools in a bag, and he was pulling his blue hood over his head. He passed Jocelin without a sign and hurried into the north transept.

'Come back!'

The old wound in the north transept had become a door, and it slammed shut. Who came back was the precentor, claiming a moment of conversation with such deadly calm it was clear he was furiously angry. But what with the dead woman, the present impossibility of prayer, and the defection of a workman, Jocelin could only put his hands to his ears and rock himself.

'It's necessary. It's an overriding necessity that I should abandon everything else to stay with these men. They have no faith and they need me. Divide responsibility for all else among you. I shall be here, every moment, in the new building.'

He peered up to where the tower started and never noticed when the precentor went away. He hurried to the master builder's side.

'Now you shall have me always with you.'

Roger Mason looked at him over the iron collar out of dull eyes.

'Good, My Lord Dean. Oh *very* good.'

Jocelin remembered the precentor and cried after him.

'You heard that, my Lord?'

And the pillars continued to sing. He girded himself and climbed up and up into the tower. Where he found men, he spoke to them cheerfully and laughed, so that they laughed back, somewhat uncertainly. They spoke to him of the long rope and how it was haunted, so that in the end, he examined it himself. It was haunted indeed. It fell down through the tower, through the wide louvre left above the crossways, and the end lay on the pavement like a dead snake. He watched the timbers of the octagons go up by this rope for reassembly. He heard the men at ground level faintly answering the halloos from above, and then the load slid up the air with not another word said. At some point in the ascent, no matter how carefully the men hauled, the rope would start to circle and snake, rubbing the sides of the louvre, so that to haul the burden through was a matter of exact judgement, lest it should strike and smash stone.

He saw Roger Mason come climbing up to the base of the tower; heard Rachel below him shouting instructions from her maximum height. This made him remember the swallow's nest so that he climbed breathlessly above where it had been. He spoke aloud to his angel.

'She never came this high.'

But the workmen heard, misunderstood him and laughed.

'No. This high, he's free of her.'

Then Jehan looked down at the climbing master builder and made the workmen snigger like the boys of the songschool.

'One day, she'll go with him even into the privy.'

That was the day that Jocelin made another discovery; Roger Mason had taken to drink. After that he watched him closely and found he was not so much in drink as soaked with it. His breath was visible, almost. He nipped here and there on the way up, or standing on a ladder, or squatting in the lee of the rising cone that was the skin of the spire. When he understood this, Jocelin had a moment of panic, like a passenger in a ship with a drunken master, but it passed. From that moment he took no account of anyone who habitually worked and lived at ground level.

The pillars continued to sing; and the news filtered through to Jocelin at this time that they were the only things that sang in the whole building. The services had moved out and were held indignantly in the bishop's palace. Sometimes, when he hurried from his house to the building he would cross the path of a Person; but he never had any trouble. The Person would do nothing but watch him stonily out of sight. Even when Father Adam told him that the Nail and the Visitor was coming he only said, vaguely — 'Visitor?' — and climbed out of sight.

His presence in the tower did the master builder no good. There was a steady inevitability about his drinking now, that was like a process in nature. Sometimes he would be sullen, cursing filthily to get a job done. When Jocelin was near, he would blaspheme in such terms as drove the white body out of Jocelin's head. Then he would go and sit in a corner with his hands over his ears to shut out the cursing, and the girl would come back, or he would remember how her feet had made a golden maze in the close and the church and the market; and he would moan behind his hands.

'She's dead. Dead!'

Sometimes by contrast, Roger would be falsely and sillily jovial, and try to force drink on anyone near. But most of the time he was just painful and slow, going heavily on the ladders; and when work was finished for the day he would lower himself to where Rachel locked his collar on and led him away. Then Jocelin would nod to himself, and say wisely:

'He doesn't care if he lives or dies.'

All the same, when she haunted him next day and he bound himself to Roger to be rid of her, he found he had misjudged him. Roger must care whether he lived or died otherwise the fear would not have laid so obvious a hand on him. There was no clear way of explaining why the fear was so obvious in the master builder. Jocelin saw it in the same way as he had seen the tent and the chain; and he saw that the fear was not a rational one, like the fear of a healthy animal. It was a poisoned fear like Roger's old fear of heights. Now it set him gripping and looking close, and enduring the heights because he had to. He doesn't mind if he dies, thought Jocelin, indeed, he would like to die; but yet he fears to fall. He would welcome a long sleep; but not at the price of falling to it. That's another reason why he goes nip-nipping from one level to another, a nip here, a nip there, with hot, stinking breath.

Thus there were a few men working at the base of the spire, one, a drunk; one, keeping his eyes averted from ground level where the golden maze of her feet was spread below him; the others, sane, more or less. There was also a mad, wooden floor at the top of the tower; and because this was a madness which might be understood, it drew Jocelin, who had seen none like it in the shed by the north transept. It was something to attend to, drawing out the mind. The octagon that lay on the floor was interrupted by grooves at even spaces, and each groove had a wedge in it. The men had assembled a second octagon above it, which rested on the wedges; and there was a cable strong enough to hold a ship, which went right round the lower octagon and bound the wedges in. When he asked Roger what this was for, he got nothing but a mouthful of curses, so he went back to a corner and brooded on his own affairs. Then one evening when Roger had gone grumbling down the ladders, Jocelin drew Jehan aside and pointed to the wedges.

'Explain this work to me.'

But Jehan laughed in his face.

'It's mad.'

Jocelin shook him by the shoulders as in the old days.

'I must know. It's my work too.'

Then Jehan shrugged under his hands so that he took them away.

'The whole thing rests on wedges. He'll pin the wood-work into the capstone. If a storm blows up before that — topple, bang, smash! If not, he'll slacken the cable little by little and let the octagons, or the members between them, stretch down. The whole thing'll hang, and hold the spire against the wind. So.'

He kicked one of the wedges.

'He thinks the whole thing will stretch — that much. Who knows? He may be right.'

'Have you seen it done before?'

Jehan laughed.

'Has anyone built this high before?'

Jocelin looked at the stone skin round them.

'Perhaps in foreign countries. They tell stories.'

'If the skin doesn't crumble, or the capstone split; if the wood stretches enough and if the pillars stand it —'

He kicked a wedge again, shook his head, and whistled ruefully.

'No one but he could have an idea like that.'

'Roger?'

'He's drunk and he's crazy. But then, you have to be crazy to build as high as this.'

He turned and began to clamber down through the trap. After a second or two, his parting words came back up the ladder.

'Up here, we're *all* crazy.'

Then Jocelin had some insight into the master builder. I must give him what strength I have, he thought. So the next morning he kept close to Roger and questioned him.

'What's this thing called, my son? And this?'

But Roger Mason would have none of him. In the end he shouted back.

'What's what? There aren't any names for bits of stone and wood. That thing fits on that thing, which'll fit on that thing — perhaps. Leave me alone!'

So he climbed heavily away like a bear, and stopped halfway up the ladder for a nip. But Jocelin went after him, not to be with the master builder, but to squat among the workmen at the top where he knew he was welcome. At first he could not understand why he was welcome, but at last he found that he was a specific against fear; and this he was able to understand fully since his angel was now in daily and nightly attendance and performed the same office for him, which was good, though it bent his back a little. Nowadays he would come back into the church at dawn, and stand, as it were, in the middle of his adult life. If the work had not yet begun, and if he could avoid the golden maze, he would stand and try to examine the extraordinary tides of feeling that were swallowing him up.

What's this called? And this?

146

Sometimes, standing in the dim church, he would put propositions to himself, though the spire in his head prevented him from coming to a conclusion.

'When it's finished I shall be free.'

Or: 'It's part of the cost, you see.'

Or: 'I know Anselm as a person; and him; and him. But I never knew her. It would be so precious to me if —'

What's this called? And this?

Once, in the grey light, when he felt calm for a whole hour, he had a thought which seemed like a blank wall; and then significant as a birthday to a child. He was looking towards the wooden screen between him and the Lady Chapel. He was remembering certain things that had happened to him and they seemed to have happened in another life.

There was God!

So he stood there, looking at the grey pillars and the grey light through the preaching patriarchs in the clerestory. Then he spoke to the wooden screen.

'Is that included?'

But there was no answer; so he hurried forward to the ladders, got there at the same time as the workmen, and gave them his blessing. And then the spire put the thoughts out of his head.

But to work now in the narrowing spire, was to be lifted a further stage from the earth. It was a beginning, not an end. The lines of the tower drew together downwards now, so that the whole thing was not massively based, but an arrow shot into the earth, with up here, an ungainly butt. The perceptible swaying was no longer soulclutching as it had been, to the men who lived in the air; but there was in the rhythmic heaviness and lightness a kind of drain, not so much on the muscles as on the

147

spirit. Jocelin learnt how the strain built up, so that after a time you would find you had held your breath, and clutched at something with frozen violence. Then you would let this breath out in a gasp, and be easy for a while, until the strain built itself up once more. But there was an advantage in working so high, three hundred feet up. When the wind blew, you could not hear the pillars singing, though you could think of them down there; four needles stuck in the earth, holding up this world of wood and stone.

The remedy for this was work which needed extreme concentration. The skin of the cone had to be built with the utmost accuracy, since only then would it achieve its full strength. Yet except on a windless day, a level placed on the flooring at the top of the tower would exhibit a kind of slow insanity, drifting about like a soul in limbo. After that, the master builder would speak to no one, but brood; and sometimes fly out at a workman.

Then another thing happened to which no one could put a name. It happened slowly like a drop in the temperature of the air. This was, perhaps, the consciousness that now they were where no men had ever been before. No one could positively detect a new law, a new menace; yet some new apprehension lay clammily on the skin. There was seldom measured speech in the cone now; silence, or muttered argument, or sudden spats of temper. Sometimes there were gusts of laughter. Now and then, there were tears.

There were also defections. Ranulf was one of these. He was small, and dry and wrinkled. He was one of the silent ones, perhaps because his English was so uncouth no one could understand more than a quarter of it. He worked with snail slowness, but he never stopped. Nor did the bursts of hysterical laughter or anger include him.

He was often forgotten; but when you looked that way again, you saw that another stone was in position with his mark on it. But one afternoon in July, when the spire was moving again, he backed away from the skin and began to put his tools in his bag. No one said anything; but one by one the others stopped too, until they were all watching him. This made no difference at all to Ranulf, who did exactly as he had done any number of times before. He arranged his tools methodically, cleaning them, and binding them with rag. He checked over his food bag, and dusted his hands. Then he took both bags and moved slowly down the cone out of sight. The others watched his head disappear, then one by one, returned to their work; but there was a cold comment in this methodical withdrawal by such a man that set limbs quivering.

There was a more terrifying defection still.

The model of the spire had been finished with a button in which the toy cross was fixed. When Jocelin first saw this button outside the north transept in its wooden cradle, he went through incredulity to a flash of terror. The button was bigger than a millstone, must weigh more than a horse and cart; yet it had to be hauled, foot by foot, to the top. He watched how they moved the stone to the crossways, then in a curtain of ropes up through the vaulting, up, stage by stage. At each stop, there was much manoeuvring with wedges and crows to the exact point for a new journey; until the capstone lay brutally dominating the centre of the first octagon. Nor was this all; for as the stone rose, there came the point where the next octagon would be too small for the stone to go through it. So three hundred and fifty feet up, they shifted the stone outside the cone on to scaffolding specially built for it. After that, the next course of the cone took the scaffolding and the stone up with them. Then the scaffolding would be removed from below, to be used again higher up, the way children play the hand game.

Jocelin found the capstone ungood to look at. As it lay, chocked and wedged and bound on the scaffolding, it hid a whole parish of the city. Moreover it hung, impossibly as Mahomet's tomb, off centre. When the swaying began in the warm, summer wind, though the soul had faith, the body became a thing of contracted muscles, quivering nerves, that believed the thing would snap those four needles down there like alder sticks. Then the only thing to do was to avert the mind and concentrate attention on the cone that rose towards the point up there, fifty feet higher; until the mind tired, and looking again, the eyes saw how a whole parish was hidden. Nor was there now the same frightened pleasure in looking down, for the inside of the cone was darkening as the skin drew together. And if the eye was indeed drawn down outside the skin to the pinnacles that reached up and out from the birdhaunted tower top, it risked lining up some stone with a point on the blue cup of earth and detecting a movement, or inventing one. Nor could his hands work. He could only crouch, clinging to his will, or whatever will it was and try to hold up the spire and the men with it, in the new, clammy place.

Perhaps this was why he found climbing so difficult. The ladders made him breathless, so that often he would arrive, to lie gasping on the planks until his heart was steady, or as steady as it normally was. The climb with hands and feet, and the comfort of the angel, was bending his back. He kept out of the way as much as possible, but this was not easy now the cone was drawing together. Yet no one at the top ever tried to drive him off, and he could not think why this was, until one day he asked Jehan who answered him simply.

'You bring us luck.'

It was Jehan who fathered the next crisis and the next defection. He came up one day, with a set, unlaughing face, borrowed the master builder's plumb and line. Then while the others snatched their midday meal in the lee of the skin, while the master builder nip-nipped and said nothing, Jehan went back quickly down the spire.

After that, the meal was very silent.

Presently Jehan came up again, handed the plumb and coil of line to the master builder, then looked at Jocelin. There was that in his face which had to be met and known. Jocelin heard his voice crack in the high giggle as he used it.

'Well? Are they sinking?'

Heavy, pause, light, pause.

Jehan licked his lips. There was a dirty green tinge round them. His voice when it came, was a croak.

'Bending.'

Then there was silence, except for the susurration of the wind over the raw edge of the cone.

The next sound was so strange, it seemed there was a new person, or a new creature in the cone. It was a mooing; and it came from Roger Mason. He was crouched in the lee of the skin, and he was looking straight through the other side.

'Roger!'

Heavy, pause.

'My son!'

Light, pause.

The master builder scrambled sideways over the boards like a crab and fumbled his way out of sight. They heard him going down, ladder after ladder; and as he sank away from them, only the moo-ing went higher, until it was a screaming and a singing, like the singing of the stones. After that, there was silence again.

Then suddenly they were all laughing, shrieking, howling, thumping stone or wood with fists that bled; and there was a great fire of love that flamed from the one to the other in the darkening cone. The will itself opened Jocelin's lips and promised them more money among the flames of love; and they hugged the lean body that was the vessel of the will.

After that he found it even easier to ignore ground-level; and this was necessary because with the bending of the pillars, people at groundlevel tended to interrupt him, and all he could do was to look through them at the spire and wait till they went away. In this trance of will, he heard how the city people cursed him for ending the services in the cathedral. Even the godless cursed him. They would stand at the west door, peer the length of the nave at the pillars. When he came through from a struggle between his angel and his devil, if they were there, they would not dare to curse him openly, but they muttered at his back. He knew what they said because he could detect the bending of the pillars himself. There was no doubt that Jehan had been right. Solid stone could not do this; but solid stone was doing it. If you looked through the nave at the east windows you could see the two nearer pillars at the crossways perceptibly bent in towards each other, though your eye had to look long and carefully. There was only one good thing to this bending. The more the pillars bent the less they sang. By midsummer, they seemed to have stopped bending and singing altogether; but Jehan said they were waiting for the gales of autumn, when he person-ally would take care to be somewhere else. This care was taken already by everyone but the builders and the man who brought them luck.

At the top, the work speeded up, as if each man felt the gales of autumn already promised on his cheek. Jocelin knew these men better than he had ever known anybody in his life, from the dumb man, to Jehan. He was part of the crew. Clinging, crouching in the lee of the skin, his angel always at his back, he began to handle wood and stone, to lay his hand to a rope, or his weight to the end of a crow. As for the men, they called him 'Father' but they treated him jocularly, like a child. As the skin came further in, and there was laughter and fierceness in the tent-like space, they let him take charge of the metal sheet that threw reflected light into the interior. He was very proud of this, even to tears, though he could not tell why. He would squat there holding the sheet, and the master carpenter would be lying on his back and hammering up into a corner.

'Left a bit, Father!'

'Like that, my son?'

'More. More. Steady!'

So he would squat there, devotedly directing the light. They are all good men, he thought. They blaspheme and curse and work with their hands, but they are good men. I taste their goodness here in the sunlight nearly four hundred feet above the pavement. Perhaps it's because they were chosen just as I was chosen.

So he told them about his angel and they were not surprised, but looked into the space behind his back and nodded soberly. Then he broke even a little more of his purpose and told them about his vision, because it seemed to him that they were worthy of this hire. But they could not understand. In the end he gave up, shaking his head and muttering fretfully.

'I have it all written down somewhere.'

After that he remembered the sermon he was going to preach when the spire was finished, and the pulpit built against the pillars he would preach it from. But at that, the others made long faces. Jehan said that any man who worked under those pillars from now on was a fool, and enough was enough. But the dumb man came to Jocelin, humming and nodding and tapping himself on the chest. So that was an end of what looked like a difficulty.

One day, the men knocked off early and would not go on no matter how much Jocelin begged them to. They simply shut him out from among them and went away. So after a while he went down too, and what with the cathedral people at groundlevel it was difficult to keep the spire erect in his head. He looked at the curved pillars, and wandered round the church until the silence and the golden marks of feet drove him back to the ladders. He climbed them again, and the flimsier ladders that were lashed among the octagons. Because he knew this time there was nothing to be done but wait, he went slowly and noted how even that made his heart trot. But he reached the top at last and squatted there among the ravens. While the sun sank in great stillness he sat there, and all the spire was in his head.

Yet before the sun had gone, he found he was not alone with his angel. Someone else was facing him. This creature was framed by the metal sheet that stood against the sky opposite him. For a moment he thought of exorcism, but when he lifted his hand, the figure raised one too. So he crawled across the boards on hands and knees and the figure crawled towards him. He knelt and peered in at the wild halo of hair, the skinny arms and legs that stuck out of a girt and dirty robe. He peered in closer and closer until his breath dimmed his own image and he had to smear it off with his sleeve. After that he knelt and peered for a long time. He examined his eyes, deep in sockets over which the skin was dragged — dragged too over the cheekbones, then sucked in. He examined the nose like a beak and now nearly as sharp, the deep grooves in the face, the gleam of teeth.

The kneeling image cleared his head. Well Jocelin, he said soundlessly to the kneeling image; Well Jocelin, this is where we have come. It began when we were knocked down, I think. It was when the earth moved, more or less. We can remember what happened since then, but what happened before is some sort of dream. Except for the vision.

After that, he got up and began to move about, restlessly. The evening turned green over the rim of the cup. Then the rim went black and shadows filled it silently so that before he was well aware of it, night had fallen and the faint stars come out. He saw a fire on the rim and guessed it was a haystack burning; but as he moved round the rim of the cone, he saw more and more fires round the rim of the world. Then a terrible dread fell on him for he knew these were the fires of Midsummer Night, lighted by the devilworshippers out on the hills. Over there, in the valley of the Hanging Stones, a vast fire shuddered brightly. All at once he cried out, not in terror but in grief. For he remembered his crew of good men, and he knew why they had knocked off work and where they were gone. So he shouted aloud in anger at someone.

'They are good men! I say so!'

But this was only one feeling. Inside them, his mind knew what it knew.

'It's another lesson. The lesson for this height. Who

could have foreseen that this was part of the scheme? Who could know that at this height the thing I thought of as a stone diagram of prayer would lift up a cross and fight eye to eye with the fires of the Devil?'

Then the workmen came back into his head, and the woman with the golden pattern of her feet, and he wept bitterly without knowing what he wept for unless it was the sins of the world. At last, when his eyes were dry, he sat gazing drearily over the rim to where the bale fires leapt.

Slowly his mind came back to its own life. If David could not build the temple because he had blood on his hands, what is to be said of us, and of me? Then the terrible christening leapt into his eye and he cried out; and then, just when he had put it away again, a host of memories flew together. He watched, powerless to stop as they added to each other. They were like sentences from a story, which though they left great gaps, still told enough. It was a story of her and Roger and Rachel and Pangall and the men. He was staring down — down past the ladders, the floors of wood, the vaulting, down to a pit dug at the crossways like a grave made ready for some notable. The disregarded bale fires shuddered round the horizon, but there was ice on his skin. He was remembering himself watching the floor down there, where among the dust and rubble a twig with a brown, obscene berry lay against his foot.

He whispered the word, in the high, dark air.

'Mistletoe!'

So at last, he tried to pray again; but she came, treading the golden maze with bowed head and billowing dress, and the bale fires shuddered round them both. He groaned, out of his terror.

'I am bewitched.'

He went halting down the ladders, without seeing them; and the story, with the disjunct sentences, burned before his mind; and at the crossways, the replaced paving stones were hot to his feet with all the fires of hell.

CHAPTER NINE

~~~∞~~~

After that he no longer laughed with the men but exhorted them. He found that though they could neither feel nor see his angel they drew some comfort from it; and that way, August came in and went out, and the spire drew towards its end. They needed the comfort of his angel, in those days, since the wind began to blow. There was one August gale from the south west that set the spire swaying like a mast; but though the pillars were bent, they did not break. It was during that gale that Father Adam told him the Lady Alison would write no more; but was coming to see him.

The gale never went away completely. It left rough weather, rain first, then a clear day, then rain again; and just when September might have brought a week's fine weather to finish the work in, it produced a sky of great height as though it were about to reveal the dimensions of the storm that was to follow. So all that time the men wrestled and swore at the capstone and the wind plucked at them; and Jocelin searched the dull reaches of the river towards the sea for a glimpse of the Holy Nail; and in his mind it came shining and powerful out of the glow of Rome where the bishop still was. He thought that perhaps the weather knew something of all this and was making haste, for it began to squeeze bursts of rain out of the air like slingshot, so that although the men were wet, they were warm with the stinging. That was how they set the capstone in place with the wind turning their tunics over their heads. For two days, with the spire vibrating, they dismantled scaffolding, left nothing but the few members for the final placing of the cross with the Nail in a box at its base. On the first of those days, Jocelin saw the Nail fifteen miles away — a long, straggling procession from village to village. But before the day was out, clouds were moving below them so he could no longer see the procession and the Visitor. All the time he exhorted the men, with rain running down his naked legs, and the wind pushing. When all was done, they dropped down into the warmth of the inside, down the shuddering ladders to the enclosed floor at the top of the tower. Jehan pushed them into place, and gave each man a maul. Then there was a long pause, the men with their mauls by the wedges, and Jehan eyeing the whole mechanism.

He turned to Jocelin at last.

'We should have more men.'

'Get them then.'

'Where?'

Then there was a pause. The dumb man hummed gently from his empty mouth. Jehan looked at the windlass.

'If we don't do it now, it'll be too late.'

He went to the windlass, unbent the fastenings, gave the bar a half turn and stopped, cocking his ear at the wooden dunce's cap in the spire above them, the whole hundred and fifty feet of it. The cable still ran ironfast round the octagon, binding the wedges against all the weight of wood.

'Tap the wedges. Gently!'

There was no new noise except the tapping. He gave the bar another half turn.

'Tap them again.'

He walked round, beating his hands together.

'I just don't know. I don't know. He ought to be here, the fat bastard!'

The bar hummed and the cable leapt. The cone of wood gave a splintering grind that turned to a shriek; then the octagon came down and the wedges shot sideways like plum stones from between thumb and finger. The crash when the octagon hit the bed went beyond thunder, was physical in the ear; and the tower bounced under foot. Jocelin fell on his knees, and among all the noises of rearrangement he heard the howling descent where the others were fighting their way down the ladders. The cone racked, splinters and dust and stone chips danced over the boards. Above his head the cone warped agonisingly and tore and split. He knelt there, hugging himself while the cone subsided to a groaning and occasional shriek of wood. Then the sound of the wind took over; but now it had other instruments to play on and experimented with them. Each movement of the spire sounded them and they were not in concert.

At last he knelt upright. Only a little while now, he thought, and I shall have peace. I must get the Nail.

Then he went to the ladder and clambered down it.

But there was no peace, even at the bottom of the corkscrew stair. It was as if the slackening of the cable had been accompanied by the tightening of another. This one was round his chest. He thought: I know what it is. It's become a race between me and the Devil. We're going faster, both of us, racing for the line. But I shall win.

He stood on the pavement of the crossways. He

listened for a while and the cable tightened as he heard the beast pawing at the windows of the clerestory, trying to get in. But now there was more than one. They were legion. They were everywhere outside, they tried the doors and windows, as if mustering and planning the final assault. So he knew the need for haste and he hurried away into the cloisters. But the Chapter met him there, disorganised, clamouring and crowded.

'Where is It?'

But instead of giving it to him, they pressed round him, and laid hands on him, speaking and even shouting, incomprehensibly. Someone pulled the skirt of his gown back and down so that it hung as in the old days. He felt hands that smoothed his hair and he understood what they wanted. So he shouted back at them.

'I shall say nothing more until you give It to me.'

Then there was comparative quiet, except for the noise of the choir boys from the other side of the cloisters, so that he had time to look the Persons over, and the Vicars Choral, and the Deputies. They are as bad as the army, he thought; only there aren't any men among them with the same courage.

The devils whispered in the high branches of the cedar.

Then Father Anonymous gave It to him in a silver box, and he received It kneeling on his knees so that some of the others knelt too. But he pressed It against the cable that lay round his chest, hurried into the choir and laid It on the High Altar, where It burned brightly in the box and there was a song round It; only he could not hear the words. He said to the Nail 'Oh be quick!', for he knew that when It was driven he would have peace. So he went back to where they were waiting for him. He looked them over from inside the cable and he saw that there were many new faces; or rather that they were the old faces, now seen in a new light. They had been busy during the last year at groundlevel. They went in new pairs and trios. They had not as he had (and the devils whimpered) complications in their heads, but many small things which was why life was easy for them. Moreover they were small themselves, and growing smaller as he watched them.

He heard Anselm speak softly.

'Why shouldn't he see him as he is?'

After that, there was a pause, while the crowd of them became smaller than the smallest children of the choir. Then these children began to rearrange themselves. They took little shuffling steps to one side or the other, but always their faces watched him as though they would like to see inside his head. They formed themselves into two ranks leading away from him so that they left a path; and the great doors of the chapter house were at the other end of it. He looked at the doors. He thought to himself; The Visitor will understand that I have become a workman, a stone mason, a carpenter, because it was necessary.

They opened one leaf of the door for him and he went through. He stood inside, and looked up at the windows where the devils were pawing. But he knew it was unimportant if they should make an entry here. So he was free to look down again; and there was the commission, ranged behind a long table covered with documents; seven men of full stature. So he went forward and knelt beside the chair set for witnesses and gave his name.

'Jocelin. Dean of the Cathedral Church of Our Lady.'

All seven men were watching him. The two secretaries had looked up from writing, the feathers lying back from their hands. The Visitor himself had half-risen from his chair, and was leaning forward, his hands on the table. He was a darkfaced man, deeply lined, shaggy about the eyebrows, his eyes set far back in his head. His robes of black and white fell round him amply. He examined Jocelin for a while, then courteously indicated the chair. Jocelin stood up and bowed; and the commission stood up and bowed like the crest of a wave. He sat in the chair as they sank again; and he said nothing, but watched their heads nodding and muttering together.

At last the Visitor turned back to him.

'It's not the proper procedure, My Lord. But perhaps —'

'Ask what you like, and I shall answer.'

'Of course.'

The Visitor smiled suddenly. He understands, thought Jocelin inside the cable. He is on my side, and he is full size.

But the Visitor was speaking again.

'Perhaps, as a preliminary, it would simplify things.'

Simplify things, thought Jocelin. If that's what he wants, I can help him.

'They think I'm mad.'

Then there was silence again, while he inspected his mind, and gave up. He nodded solemnly at the Visitor.

'Perhaps I am.'

Their heads went together again. After all, he thought, I haven't simplified things, I've complicated them. He groaned and put up a hand to his head and felt something in his hair. He pulled out a curled shaving, bent it over his fingers, stretched it till it snapped, then threw the pieces away. One of the secretaries, nodding, got up out of the mutter, bowed quickly and hurried away.

The Visitor spoke again, gently.

163

'We had drawn up a list of questions, taken from the representations and depositions.'

'Representations? Depositions?'

'But surely you knew? Some of them are dated from as much as two years ago!'

He examined the two years.

'I've been preoccupied.'

The Visitor was smiling openly now.

'Some of the questions are irrelevant in the circumstances, I think. For example, the matter of the candles.'

'What candles?'

The Visitor was examining a document that had been passed to him. There was a curious note in his voice.

'This Person appears to believe that Holy Church has suffered a mortal blow because for two years the faithful haven't been burning candles in the nave of the Cathedral.'

'Anselm!'

'He's your Sacrist, isn't he? He appears to derive a significant proportion of his income from the sale of candles; though of course his prime objection is on a much loftier and spiritual plane. Yes. Father Anselm, a Principal Person, and Lord Sacrist of the Cathedral Church of Our Lady. He has a personal seal.'

'Anselm!'

(Going away, diminishing, vanishing backwards down a long tunnel —)

'My Lord Dean. Perhaps we should see our way more clearly if you would assent to or dissent from certain general — accusations.'

'I said ask what you like.'

'Indeed I shall, My Lord.'

The Visitor shuffled documents. Jocelin waited, hands clasped before his chest, as he inspected the row of sandals under the table. Presently the Visitor looked up.

'Would you agree that the, what is referred to here as "The Rich Fabric of Constant Praise", has been unnecessarily interrupted?'

Jocelin nodded emphatically.

'It's true. How true it is! So true!'

'Explain then.'

'Before we began to build, we sealed off the east end as best we could, and held the services in the Lady Chapel.'

'It's the common practice.'

'So at that time the services continued. But later, you see, men felt there was some danger. When the pillars began to sing, and then bend, there was none of the chapter, none of the laity, no one who dared to worship there.'

'In fact, the services of the church came to an end?'

Jocelin looked up quickly and spread his hands.

'No. Not if you can see — all the complications. I was there, all the time. It was a kind of service. I was there, and they were there, adding glory to the house.'

'They?'

'The workmen. There were fewer and fewer of them of course; but some stayed right to the end.'

The Visitor said nothing; but he felt himself understood, and hurried on.

'I don't know what names and seals — except one — are affixed to those documents you have there, nor what the complaints are, except in general terms. All I know is, I looked for men of faith to be with me; and there was none.'

He saw the Visitor found it a good and unexpected answer. All at once, before the friendly face, he was overcome with a passion to explain everything.

'You see, there were three sorts of people. Those who ran, those who stayed, and those who were built in. Pangall —'

'Ah yes. Pangall.'

'She's woven into it everywhere. She died and then she came alive in my mind. She's there now. She haunts me. She wasn't alive before, not in that way. And I must have known about him before, you see, down in the vaults, the cellarage of my mind. But it was all necessary, of course. Like the money.'

'We must examine the question of money for a moment. Is this your seal? And this?'

'I suppose so. Yes.'

'Are you wealthy?'

'No.'

'How are these to be paid then?'

'As He supported the pillars and provided the Nail.'

There it came again, the notsong, the absence of re-membering, the overriding thing — He saw without interest, the secretary steal back to his place, and saw that Father Anonymous was standing behind and a little to one side of the chair set for witnesses. He heard the devils paw and rattle at the windows. He ran in his mind to get to the spire before them.

'My Lord, while we talk here, it may fall. Let me take It now, and drive It in!'

The Visitor was looking at him intently, under his thick eyebrows.

'You believe that the spire, for want of a nail —'

Jocelin held up his hand quickly, to stop the Visitor. Frowning, he strove to catch the song, so nearly teeter-ing on the edge of memory; but it faded away, as Anselm had faded. He looked up, to see the Visitor leaning back, and smiling strangely.

166

'My Lord Dean, I have nothing but respectful admiration for your faith.'

'Mine?'

'You spoke of a woman. Who is she? Our Lady?'

'Oh no! Indeed no! Nothing like that. She was his wife, Pangall's. After I found the mistletoe berry you see —'

'When was this?'

The question was hard and sharp as the edge of stone. He saw that the seven men had stopped every movement, and were looking at him intently, soberly, as if he were on trial.

That's it, he thought. Why didn't I think of it before? I'm on trial.

'I don't know. I can't remember. A long time ago.'

'What did you mean about people being "built in"?'

He held his head in his hands, shut his eyes and swayed from side to side.

'I don't know. There aren't enough words. The complications —'

Then there was a long silence. At last he opened his eyes, and saw that the Visitor had relaxed again, and was smiling kindly like a friend.

'We must get on, My Lord Dean, I believe. These workmen who stayed with you to the end. Were they good men?'

'Oh yes!'

'*Good* men?'

'Very good, very good indeed!'

But papers were being shuffled on the long table. The Visitor took one and began to read from it, in an unemotional voice.

' "Murderers, cutthroats, rowdies, brawlers, rapers, notorious fornicators, sodomites, atheists, or worse." '

'I — No.'

The Visitor was looking at him over the paper.

'Good men?'

Jocelin struck his right fist into the palm of the other.

'They were bold men!'

The Visitor let out his breath in sudden exasperation. He threw the paper on to a pile.

'My Lord. What's at the bottom of all this?'

Jocelin embraced the plain question thankfully.

'It was so simple at first. On the purely human level of course, it's a story of shame and folly — Jocelin's Folly, they call it. I had a vision you see, a clear and explicit vision. It was *so* simple! It was to be my work. I was chosen for it. But then the complications began. A single green shoot at first, then clinging tendrils, then branches, then at last a riotous confusion — I didn't know what would be required of me, even when I offered myself. Then later, he and she —'

'This vision.'

'I have it written down in a notebook in the bottom left hand corner of my chest. You can read it if that would help. Soon I shall preach a sermon — we shall have a new pulpit built at the crossways; and then everyone —'

'You are trying to say that the vision made your building of the spire an overriding necessity?'

'Exactly so.'

'And that from this vision, or revelation — which would you call it?'

'I'm not a learned man. Forgive me.'

'From this vision, everything else followed?'

'Just so, just so.'

'To whom did you confide it?'

'To my confessor, of course.'

Outside the windows, the devils were only just invisible. He looked impatiently at the Visitor.

'My Lord. While we sit here —'

But the Visitor held up his hand. The secretary was speaking from the left end of the table.

'Anselm, My Lord. The Sacrist.'

'The man who is so concerned about his candles? He is your confessor?'

'He was, My Lord. And hers. If only you knew the pain of knowing and not knowing!'

'Then you've changed your confessor? How long since?'

'I — No, My Lord.'

'Then he's your confessor still, if you have one.'

'I suppose so. Yes.'

'My Lord Dean. When did you last go to confession?'

'I can't remember.'

'A month? A year? Two years?'

'I can't remember, I tell you!'

The questions drove him back in his chair, they pressed in, were unfair and unanswerable.

'And all this time, you have been withdrawn from your spiritual peers, keeping company with men, who if our information is correct, are more than merely wicked?'

The question loomed over him, expanded, became a mountain. He saw to what a height a mind must climb, ladder after ladder, if it were to answer, so he prepared once more to climb. He stood up, reached down his right hand, drew the hem of his gown through between his knees, twisted it, and tucked it up through his girdle.

The seven men were standing too. They were stiller than the saints that jumped and rattled in the windows.

The Visitor sank back slowly into his chair. His smile was very amiable again.

'You are exhausted by your labours, My Lord. Let us continue this discussion tomorrow.'

'But while we waste time here, they are there, outside the windows —'

'By the authority of this seal, I command you to return to your own house.'

It was gently, kindly spoken; but when he had inspected the seal, he knew that at last he had no answer. He turned to go, and the seven men bowed; but he said to himself, We have got beyond the bowing stage! He walked away over the patterned, clicking pavement, and Father Anonymous hung at his shoulder. The door shut behind him; and there were his spiritual peers ranged in the cloisters. They were a little larger now, but not much. So he walked between the rows of eyes, and he dismissed them from his mind.

By the west door, he cocked an ear and an eye to see what the devils were doing to the weather. They were free, or in the process of becoming free; and already they were doing more than enough. The storm had swung from the south east to the east, so there was a lee at the west end of the cathedral. Since the water was unblown here, it cascaded down the front from a dozen gullies, spouted from stone mouths, and washed in a constant sheet over the gravel before the steps. Yet with all that water about, the sky was high and light, and there were streaky clouds that seemed to weave over each other. The rain was not falling from any visible cloud. It came as if born from the very air — as if the air were a sponge, spurting here and there with drops that fell oddly.

But Father Anonymous was at his side.

'Come, My Lord.'

A cloak fell round Jocelin's shoulders.

'The hood, My Lord. So.'

Gently, calmly, pressure on the elbow.

'This way, My Lord, across here. Now.'

As they came out of the lee, the wind hit them, and hurried them towards the deanery. When they had reached the upper room where his bed was, he dropped the cloak from his shoulders into the chaplain's hands, and stood, looking down at the floor. The cable still bound his chest.

'I shan't sleep till it's finished.'

He turned to the window, and watched, as a bucketful of water dashed over it. He felt his angel and his devil at war behind his back.

'Go to them now, go back to them. Tell them we must drive the Nail now, before it's too late. It's a race.'

He shut his eyes, and recognised instantly the impossibility of prayer. So he opened them again, and saw Father Anonymous hesitating there.

He ordered him away irritably.

'You are still under obedience. Be gone!'

When next he looked, the little man had disappeared.

He began to pace up and down. When it is driven, he thought, then the spire and my witch will cease to haunt me. Perhaps one day I shall know how wicked she was — exactly how wicked she was; but now the spire is the thing; and the Nail.

After a while he went and stood close to the window; but he could see nothing clearly because of the drops that hung shuddering, wandered aimlessly, or disappeared as if they had been snatched. He waited for a message but none came. I said I was a fool, he thought; and it is truer than I meant. I should have gone myself — what am I

171

doing here? But he went on standing, hands clasped, lips pursing and unpursing, while the light faded in the window and the wind boomed on. When the window was no more than a dull rectangle, he found how tired he was of standing; so he went to his bed and lay on it fully dressed and waiting. Once he heard a crash and clatter from somewhere among the roofs of the deanery and started up. After that, he lay flat no longer, but listened, propped on one elbow in the thick darkness. He saw the spire fall a hundred times — heard it fall a hundred times until the gale beat in his very head. He tried to doze but could not tell which was sleeping and which waking since both were the same nightmare. He tried to think of other things, only to find that the spire was so firmly based in his head there was nothing else to think of. Sometimes the wind would drop for a moment and his heart would bound; but always the wind would return with a lashing of shot on the window, and at last it roared without ceasing.

So he lay and dozed or waked. At some point in the night the window leaped into bright light so that his body contracted on the bed, but the noise of thunder never penetrated the wind. After that there were more crashes among the roofing, and the skitter of tiles. Then it occurred to him that if he watched at the window he might see how the building did, by the lightning flash when it came, so he crawled off his bed and stood waiting. The next flash showed him nothing but that the window was in the wrong place; so he turned a little and finally made out the dim square. He went close, put his face by it, listening to the slung water and then the next flash came. It was not even the split of a glimpse. It was a pain in the eyes, with light turning green even after he had got his hands in front of them. He knew that the

172

bulk in the middle of the light was the tower but could not tell exactly how it was shaped, or whether it leaned, or whether it had a spire on. He fumbled back to his bed and lay on it. He lay on his face, trying, of all things, to think of old times that had been happy; times with Father Anselm, master of the novices or novice rather, in the sunlit place by the sea; and then again, he got up and stood by the window. But the next flash was far away beyond the cathedral so that he seemed to see its black bulk hurtling shapelessly at him. Then he lay down again and did not know whether he fell into a doze or whether he fainted clean away.

He came up out of a deep well. There was a flat noise at the top like a cover; but this was not what drew him up. There were other noises, thin screams, bird noises, almost. Suddenly he was wide awake, knowing where he was, in the dimmest of grey lights. He could hear their clamour on the stairs.

He rolled off the bed and went quickly to the door.

'I'm here. You must be brave, my children!'

But the voices shrieked and sobbed.

'— now and in the hour of —'

'— Father!'

He shouted down the stairs.

'No harm is coming to you!'

There were hands at his feet, and pulling at his gown.

'The city's being destroyed!'

'— the whole thatch of a house lying in the graveyard and beating to pieces —'

He shouted down at them.

'What's happened to the spire?'

Hands crawled up his body, and a beard thrust into his face.

173

'It's falling, Reverend Father. There were stones falling from the parapet even before dark —'

He pulled himself away and went to the window and rubbed at the dullness with foolish fingers as though he could smear it away like paint. He hurried back to the stairs.

'Satan is loose. But no harm shall come to you. I swear it.'

'Help us, Reverend Father! Pray for us!'

Then, in the faint light, among the hands and the booming of the wind, he saw what he had to do. He pressed forward among them, pushing them aside, pulled his skirt away, shook a hand from his elbow. Then he was clear, with a stone step coming to each foot. He found the great hall and the door with its latch. He fumbled the latch up, and the door slammed open, throwing him back across the hall. He crept round the wind and bored into it through the doorway. Again it threw him back against the wall so that he hung there, panting. Then the wind let him go from its mouth so that he dropped on gravel. He scrambled forward and the wind picked him up again, then let him fall on all fours; and already he was soaked as though he had fallen in the river. He had a confused thought that now he worked with his body as others did, and he burrowed forward across the lane to the graveyard. A handful of something struck his face and left a stinging behind as if it had been nettles. He fell in the lee of a hummock with a wooden cross on it and the skirt of his gown flogged him, so he pulled it up through his belt. A lath came from somewhere and raised a cruel welt on his thigh.

He lifted his head a little and squinted into the grey light, across the useful grave; and at that moment, Satan in the likeness of a cosmic wildcat leapt off all four

feet on the north east horizon and came screaming down
at Jocelin and his folly. The cloak burst at his throat and
went flapping away somewhere like a black crow, but his
hands held to the wooden cross. He lay there cunningly,
until the wildcat had tired a little. After that he went
from grave to grave, grabbing a cross and a lee, until he
came to the biggest lee of all by the west door, and
through the door, leaning his back against it and gasping for breath. Yet for a moment as he leaned there he
thought the cathedral had a full congregation. But then
he realised that the lights were swimming inside his
eyes, and the singing was the noise of all the devils out
of hell. They swarmed through the dim heights, they
banged and rattled and smashed at the windows in an
extravagance of fury, they made the great window at the
west end boom like a sail. But he minded them no more
than birds as they swooped at him, for he was outside
himself, awake and asleep at the same time, a man led.
Wah! Wah! they howled, and Yah! Yah! they howled,
beating at him with scaly wings then going off to batter
at the singing pillars and the windows and the vaulting
that shuddered over; and he heard someone, himself
perhaps, imitating their cries as his body ran crouching
up the nave through the semi-darkness. He could hear
the groans of the arcades as they stiffened their stone
shoulders. When he saw the deserted altar before him
the devils raged as they leapt and swung from the main
arch. He fumbled at the altar, then snatched the silver
box as if it contained nothing but an ordinary nail.
There came a smash from the south transept, the crash
and shatter of stone; from the north transept a boom and
the icy skitter of glass. The devils fought with him at the
entry to the corkscrew stairs but he beat them off with
the Nail. Then as he made his way up his heart began to

hit him at the base of the throat, and when he reached the lower chamber he could hardly see it for the glossy lights that danced round him. Nor could his ears accept the noise any more; for what had once been the whispered expostulations of the spire was now a shouting and screaming with the roar of released Satan as a sort of universal black background. Wood and stone no longer swayed subtly. They lurched so that he was flung sideways, or clung to the ladders like a man climbing a mast at sea. On one side out in the roar, there was a continual break and fall. In the tent of wood at the top of the tower, the floor was deep in broken stone and splinters, in which he scrabbled for the foot of the first of the spire ladders. There was a devil at his left who opened and shut a mouth of grey daylight slowly, as he looked. Then there were the ladders over ladder, zigzag into darkness — one ladder newly freed at the bottom, another bowed and humming as if it had been strung. The darkness was full of splinters that scratched and stabbed as he scrambled up, his angel burning and thrusting, the box twisted into the lap of his skirt — up, up, to where there was so little space the skin enclosed him like a chimney and he could feel the difference in the movement of wood and stone skin, and then, huddled in the last space of all, fumbling open the box, dropping the linen, holding the Nail workmanlike, his weight gripped by leg and elbow, banging away with the soft silver box, beating the Nail into wood, fumbling, feeling, banging —

The noises of the spire and the spire itself, moved out of his head. He let the box fall and could not hear the erratic sounds of its descent. He began to let himself down, rung by rung. He felt the hand by which he held on begin to tremble uncontrollably, so he clung with his body. By the time he had reached the corkscrew stair he was crawling.

The devils still had possession of the nave though the spire was safe from them. But he was not safe from them himself. His angel left him, and the sweetness of his devil was laid on him like a hot hand. He felt the waters of sleep rising and was powerless to prevent them. He crawled out of the stair into the grey ambulatory and lay on his face among smashed stone, and it was as if all substance was flowering softly. The devils no longer screamed, but sang. They sang softly and remorselessly. They disguised themselves and appeared in his head as people.

He spoke to the smashed stone.

'I drove the Nail. You might have fallen for want of It!'

But the devils bound him softly and they showed him a vision that drew near. All at once he was looking right across the close in sunlight to where the elms made a shade over a swarm of daisies. The devils were dancing there, three of them, sweet and small. He drew near, down a long line of shadow. They were dancing and clapping their hands and singing.

> '*For want of a nail the shoe was lost,*
> *For want of a shoe the horse was lost,*
> *For want of a horse the rider was lost,*
> *For want of a rider the kingdom was lost —*'

He heard himself, younger and laughing, finish the song for them —

'*And all for the want of a horseshoe nail!* Come here, child.'

Then the devil drew near over the grass, while the others went away and he stood looking down and loving her innocence and beauty. He heard his kind questions probing, saw her restless, hands behind her back, red hair straggled this way and that, one thin foot rubbing over the other; heard her make an answer out of her complete incomprehension —

'But it's just a game we're playing, Father!'

In this uncountry there was blue sky and light, consent and no sin. She came towards him naked in her red hair. She was smiling and humming from an empty mouth. He knew the sound explained everything, removed all hurt and all concealment, for this was the nature of the uncountry. He could not see the devil's face for this was the nature of the uncountry too; but he knew she was there, and moving towards him totally as he was moving towards her. Then there was a wave of ineffable good sweetness, wave after wave, and an atonement.

And then there was nothing.

CHAPTER TEN

~~~❦~~~

He came to himself very slowly. His cheek was on broken stone, and the daylight was inescapably present. For a long time, even after his eyes were open they were the only part of him that he moved. He sent his sight down the long corridor and saw a familiar monument. He attached himself to this, examining it inch by inch, as if this were a way of filling time, lest something worse should come to fill it. But the monument gave no help, nor did anything else. At last he was left, helplessly in the grip of the new knowledge.

That was when he spoke first.

'Of course. I should have known. I should have understood.'

There were noises in the church, the distant clash of a door, voices. He got up and limped slowly toward the crossways. When he stepped out into it, there were shouts. Two men servants came running and father Adam was behind them. He waited for the chaplain, head and hands hanging.

'What must I do?'

'Go with me. The woman is waiting.'

'What woman?'

But even as he said this, he remembered she was dead;

179

and that this woman was Alison in search of a comfortable grave.

'I'll see her. She may know something. It was her whole life, after all.'

So they went together down the nave, the two men behind them. There was a figure in her corner, and his heart moved; but it was the dumb man, not even humming. He knew how the shame included the dumb young man, and he looked away, to the door through which they led him.

He stopped in the forecourt of the deanery.

'May I still go in?'

'It was decided so. For the time being.'

He nodded, and went in over the familiar stones. But the great hall had changed like so many other things. There was a fire of logs, there were wax candles everywhere, lighted as for an altar, there was a carpet before the fire and two chairs. The chairs were hardly visible because of the brightness of the candles, and he thought how like the candles were to the glossy patches that sometimes swam before his eyes. Even so, he had not time to inspect the changes thoroughly, for the woman was sitting in the chair on the other side of the fire, with women at her back. She rose, as he came to the edge of the carpet, sank to her knees, took his hand and kissed it, murmuring.

'Reverend Father. Jocelin!'

But then without any change she got to her feet, and spoke, half-turned to the others.

'There should be hot water, towels, a comb —'

He stopped her with his hand lifted.

'It doesn't matter.'

After the silence and pause, he looked at the other women.

'Let them leave us together.'

The shadows of women withdrew; and when they had gone she took his hand in hers, pressed gently on it, sat him down in the chair; and on his left side he felt the soft warmth of the fire. He saw how tiny she was, not much larger than a child, for her face was still little above the level of his eyes. She looked past his shoulder.

'Will you send your chaplain away too, nephew?'

'He stays. I'm in his care. And even if it weren't so, I ought not to be alone with you.'

At that she laughed outright.

'Thank you for the compliment.'

But he could not understand her and did not bother to try. She nodded seriously as if she understood this.

'I forgot how provincial you'd be.'

'I?'

Provincial. Of a province, away from the centre of things, limited in vision and scope.

'It may be so.'

But there was her face a yard away, to be examined, the blandness only less white and smooth than the pearls that edged her black coif. Her hair would be black beneath it — or had been black. He examined the arched, thin eyebrows, looked into the black balls of her eyes. She began to laugh, but he cut her short querulously.

'Be still, woman!'

So she stood, smiling and obedient.

Black dress, full. Pearls also at the throat. Hand — and as if she understood what he wished, she raised it to him — plump and white. Behind the hand, her face — and again, as if she understood what he wished, she put the hand out of sight — face smiling, plump as the hand, only a little this side of fatness. A tiny mouth, nose arched. Eyelids, dark and glistening, painted perhaps, eyelashes long and thick; water now caught among the lower ones.

'My mother's sister.'

The smile became a grimace, and the water fell. Nevertheless, her voice sounded light and amused.

'The naughty one.'

All at once she was moving quickly, and there was a scrap of white stuff in her hand.

'This at least.'

She leant forward so that he caught a sudden breath of spring and shut his eyes for faintness at it. Through the thronging memories he felt the white stuff touch and smear on his cheeks, felt a hand at his hair. He heard her murmuring again.

'After all, even the —'

He opened his eyes in the perfume while she was still busy about him. He examined her face from only a few inches away; and now he saw how carefully preserved and tended it was. The smooth skin was netted down by lines too fine to be seen from further off. It was a compromise between too much fat and too little, as could be seen by the deeper lines defended from becoming wrinkles at the corner of each eye and in the bland forehead. It was a face that must defend itself by dancing from expression to expression, lest it should be still, and sag. Only the eyes, the little mouth, the nose, held out — bastions so strong they need not be defended. He felt a remote kind of pity for the face and did not know how to express it, so he muttered instead.

'Thank you, thank you.'

She let his face alone at last, took the spring away with her across the carpet, turned and sat down facing him.

'Well, nephew?'

Then he remembered that she had not come to answer a question, but to get something from him. He rubbed the side of his head.

'As for those letters you sent me, and the business of your tomb —'

She had her hands up and cried out.

'No indeed! Don't think of them!'

But he was busy again.

'The decision mayn't be mine now, though I'm not sure. Father Adam —'

He raised his voice.

'Father Adam?'

'Reverend Father? I can't hear you. Must I come closer?'

What was I going to ask him? Her?

'No matter.'

The fire was leaping in his eyes.

'Oh no, Jocelin! I came because of you — because of how you are. You must believe it!'

'You worried about me? I, the provincial?'

'Your story's known in the country. In the world, I might say.'

'There's a sense in which your body would — forgive me — defile it.'

Then he heard how quick her temper could be.

'You haven't defiled it yourself? Those men? The church empty? That stone hammer hanging up there and waiting to strike?'

He looked into the fire and answered her patiently.

'It's a hard thing for a woman to understand. I was chosen, you see. After that, I spent my life finding out what the work would be and then doing it. I offered myself. One should be much, much more careful.'

'Chosen?'

'They'll let you build a tomb there, I've no doubt. But whether I would or not — I wonder.'

'Chosen?'

'By God. He does, after all. Then I chose Roger Mason. There was no one else to do it — who could do it. Then all the rest followed.'

He looked up, startled by her laughter.

'Listen nephew. *I* chose you. No. Listen, and I'll tell you something. It wasn't at Windsor but at a hunting lodge. We were lying on the day bed together —'

'What's this to do with me?'

'I'd pleased him and he wanted to give me a present, though I had everything in the world I wanted for myself —'

'I won't hear you.'

'But then I had a thought, for I was happy and therefore generous; and so I answered; "I have a sister and she has a son." '

She was smiling again, but ruefully.

'Mind, I'll admit it wasn't just generosity. She was so, so *pious*, so dreary, and she'd always — Well, it was half-generosity, call it that. Because she was like you, in a way, stubborn, insulting —'

'Woman — what did he say?'

'Oh sit down again, Jocelin! You make me nervous, standing there like a great bird hunched in the rain. I wonder if I *was* triumphing a little?'

'*What did he say?*'

'He said : "We shall drop a plum in his mouth." Just like that. Casually. And then I said, "He's a novice, I believe, in some monastery or other." I started to giggle, and he started to roar with laughter and then we were hugging each other and rolling over and over — because you must admit, it was not without its funny side. We were both young, after all. It appealed to us. Jocelin —?'

He found she was kneeling close to him.

'Jocelin? What does it matter? It's the quality of living.'

He answered her hoarsely.

'The things I've done.'

After a while he went on.

'I always reckoned to sacrifice my life to the work; and perhaps this is the unspeakable way of doing it. And after all, there's the Nail —'

'What nail, nephew? You're so confused!'

'Our bishop Walter in Rome —'

'I know Rome. And I know bishop Walter.'

'Well there, you see. What do I matter? Only the thing matters because, because —'

'Because what?'

'There's a level you can't understand. He nailed it to the sky. I asked him for money, blind fool that I was. He did better.'

There, he thought. It's finished. But it was not, for he heard her speak again, in a breathless voice.

'You asked him for money — and he sent you a nail!'

'I said so.'

'*Walter!*'

She began to laugh, round after round of laughter that built up high, until it took away her breath, and in the silence he heard the singing of pillars in his ears. It was not that he understood anything or worked out anything by logical steps in his head; but that there was a sickness driving in and a shuddering of the body to his very fingertips. Then the sickness drowned him.

But he felt her tugging at his hands.

'Jocelin! Jocelin! Nothing matters as much as that!'

He opened his eyes.

185

'You must believe, Jocelin!'

'Believe?'

'Oh yes, yes. Believe in your — vocation — and in the nail —'

She had him by the shoulders and was shaking him.

'Listen to me. Listen I said! I wouldn't have told you if —'

'It doesn't matter.'

'You had a question for me. Think of that, concentrate on that. What was it?'

He looked into her eyes and saw how frightened she was.

'What is it that —'

But this was so like a children's guessing game that he had to finish on a high laugh.

'I remember now. What is it when one's mind turns to one thing only, and that not the lawful, the ordained thing; but to the unlawful. To brood, and remember half in pleasure, half in a kind of subtle torment —'

'What thing?'

'And when they die; for they die, they die; to recreate scenes that never happened to her —'

'Her?'

'To see her in every detail outlined against the air of the uncountry — indeed, to be able to see nothing else — to know that this is a logical part of all that went before —'

She was whispering, very near him.

'This happened to you?'

'It's a kind of haunting. All part of the rest.'

He looked at her earnestly, speaking right into her eyes.

'You'd know of course. Only tell me. That's all I want. It's witchcraft isn't it? It *must* be witchcraft!'

186

But she was withdrawing from him, leaning back, getting up, retreating across the carpet. She left the terrible whisper behind her.

'Yes. Witchcraft. Witchcraft.'

Then she had gone somewhere and he was left, nodding solemnly to the fire.

'There's a pattern in it. There's more to be destroyed. There must be more.'

He thought of Father Adam in the shadows.

'What do you think?'

'Her feet go down to hell.'

He put her away from his mind, and she vanished out of his life like a raindrop in a river.

'Confusion everywhere.'

After a while, Father Adam spoke again.

'You must sleep.'

'I shall never sleep again.'

'Come, Father.'

'I shall sit here and wait. There's a pattern, and it's not complete.'

So he sat, watching the armies of sparks that wandered through the fire. He spoke sometimes, but not to Father Adam.

'Yet it still stands.'

Then he moaned and rocked himself. Once, much later, he started up and cried out—

'Blasphemy!'

Hours later, when the fire was nothing but embers, he spoke again.

'There's a kinship among men who have sat by a dying fire and measured the worth of their life by it.'

Daylight crept through the windows and waned where the candles had guttered out. The last spark of the fire disappeared in the great hall, and the messenger came. It was the man of faith, humming and pointing. Jocelin rose carefully from his chair.

'Have I your permission to go with him, Father?'

The keeper made a little gesture of disclaim.

'We will go together.'

So Jocelin bowed his head and kept it bowed, and they went to the west door in the last flutters of disturbed air. There seemed nothing new in the nave, so Jocelin spoke sideways to the dumb man, not wishing to look him in the face.

'Show us, my son.'

Then the dumb man led them on tiptoe to the south east pillar and showed them where he had chiselled a little hole in the stone, then went away again on tiptoe. Jocelin understood what he had to do. He took the chisel with its burred-over head out of the hole, lifted up an iron probe and thrust it in. It sank in, in, through the stone skin, grated and pierced in among the rubble with which the giants who had been on the earth in those days had filled the heart of the pillar.

Then all things came together. His spirit threw itself down an interior gulf, down, throw away, offer, destroy utterly, build me in with the rest of them; and as he did this he threw his physical body down too, knees, face, chest, smashing on the stone.

Then his angel put away the two wings from the cloven hoof and struck him from arse to the head with a whitehot flail. It filled his spine with sick fire and he shrieked because he could not bear it yet knew he would have to. At some point there were clumsy hands that tried to pick him up; but he could not tell them of the flail because of the way his body threw itself round the crossways like a broken snake. So the body shrieked and the hands fought with him and under the heap was

188

Jocelin who knew that at last one good prayer had been answered.

When the pain ebbed he found they were carrying him back from the place of the sacrifice with careful hands. He lay on an absence of back, and waited. The angel with the flail could only do so much; just as much as the body could accept, whatever the head thought about it. After that there would be nothing in the back at all, no feeling whatsoever.

They laid him on his bed in the upper room, where he faced the stone ribs of the vaulting. Sometimes the angel left him so that he could think.

I have given it my back.

Him.

Her.

Thou,

Sometimes he would whisper fretfully.

'Has it fallen?'

The clothespeg man would answer him tranquilly.

'Not yet.'

One day of comparative clarity, he had a thought.

'Was it much damaged?'

'If I lift you to sit up, Father, you can see through the window.'

This made him turn his head from side to side on the pillow.

'I shall never look at it again.'

Then he knew, by the diminution of the light, that Father Adam had gone to the window.

'If you gave it a casual glance you would think it un-harmed. But the spire leans a little, threatening the cloisters. It's impacted into the parapet at the top of the tower. There's a deal of broken stone.'

For a while he lay still. He muttered.

'The next wind. The next wind.'

The clothespeg man came near, leaned over him and spoke gently. Near as this, it was possible to see that he had some kind of face.

'You make too much fuss, Father. It's a great harm, certainly, but you built in faith, however mistaken. That's a small sin, as sins go. Life itself is a rickety building.'

Then Jocelin began to turn his head from side to side again.

'What can you know, Father Anonymous? You see the outside of things. You don't know the tenth of it.'

As if he stood at Father Adam's side, rebuking sin, the angel struck again. When Jocelin came to himself, Father Adam was still there, and speaking as if no third one had interrupted them.

'Remember your faith, my son.'

My faith, thought Jocelin, what faith? But he did not say this to the face above him that one day might come into some sort of focus. Instead he gasped and laughed.

'Would you like to see my faith? It lies there, in the old chest. A little notebook in the left hand corner.'

He paused for a moment to get his breath then laughed again.

'Take. Read.'

There was a time of shift and shuffle, creaking of the lid. Then Father Adam spoke from the light of the window.

'Aloud?'

'Aloud.'

The ink must be brown, he thought. Anselm was still a young man, and Roger Mason no more than a boy. As for her — And I was young, or younger.

Father Adam scratched his voice into the evening air.

' "One evening when I had already held this position for three years, I was kneeling in my oratory, praying with what little strength I had that the pride of my position should be taken from me. I was young, and I took a monstrous pride in this great house of mine. I was all pride —" '

'Indeed I was.'

' "An infinite charity must have sided with me. I made little movements of aspiration as befitted my capacity. I strove to see the building as a thing, an object standing in my way; and this was easy, since its very walls were visible outside the window —" '

But Jocelin was turning his head from side to side, again. He thought — what does this explain? Nothing! Nothing!

Is it nothing?

' "I watched the outline of the roof, the walls, the projecting transepts, the pinnacles standing at intervals along the parapets —" '

'Was it nothing, Father?'

' "I know now why my gaze was so directed. But at the time I knew nothing, only knelt there, until watching had made me indifferent to the thing I watched. Then, my heart moved; say that a feeling rose from my heart. It grew stronger, reached up until at the utmost tip it burst into a living fire —" '

'It's true — I swear it!'

' "— which passed away, but left me now transfixed. For there, against the sky, I saw the nearest pinnacle; and it was the exact image of my prayer in stone. There was the uprush, the ornamentation of sidethoughts for others, then the rush of the heart, rising, narrowing, piercing — and at the top, still carved in stone, the thing I had felt as a flame of fire." '

'That's how it was. You can still see the pinnacle, if you turn your head.'

' "If this seemed strange to my ignorance, my children, how shall I describe the wonder of what happened next? For as I looked, my understanding spread. It was as if the pinnacle had been a key to unlock a vast book. It was as if I had acquired a new ear for hearing, a new eye to look with. For the whole building — and I, in my youthful folly, had made mouths at it! — the whole building revealed itself to me. The whole building spoke. 'We are labour' said the walls. The ogival windows clasped their hands and sang; 'We are prayer.' And the trinity of the triangular roof — but how shall I say it? I had tried to give away my house; and it had returned to me a thousand-fold." '

'Even so.'

' "I rushed across to the west door and bounded inside. Now let me be precise. I had seen the whole building as an image of living, praying man. But inside it was a richly written book to instruct that man. It was a winter's evening, I remember, and by then, the nave was darkling. Those patriarchs up there glowed in the windows and the saints below them; and at every altar in the side aisles there were nests of the candles you had given. There was a memory of incense and a mutter of mass priests from the chantries — but you have seen! I went forward, nay, was carried forward by a spiritual delight that grew with every step I took, in certainty and abnegation. By the time I was here, at the crossways, there was nothing for it but to cast myself headlong on these stones —" '

'Those same crossways. And I've done it since.'

' "For in some way I was made one with the wise, the saintly — no, the saintly and wise builders —" '

'The pillars are bending.'

' "I was initiated into their secret language, so plain, so visible for all men who can see, to see. His manual of heaven and hell lay open before me, and I could perceive my nothingness in this scheme. A new movement of my heart seemed to be building the church in me, walls, pinnacles, sloping roof, with a complete naturalness and inevitability of consent; so that in my newfound humility and newfound knowledge, a fountain burst up from me, up, out, through, up with flame and light, up through a notspace, filling with ultimate urgency and not to be denied (but who could deny — who would?) an implacable, unstoppable, glorious fountain of the spirit, a wild burning of me for Thee —" '

'Oh God!'

' "— and at the top, if top is the word, some mode, some gift that brought no pride of having. My body lay on the soft stones, changed in a moment, the twinkling of an eye, resurrected from daily life. The vision left me at last; and the memory of it, which I savoured as manna, shaped itself to the spire, fitted into a shape, the centre of the book, the crown, the ultimate prayer!" '

'It's an ungainly, crumbling thing. Nothing like. Nothing at all.'

' "So at last I got to my feet. The candles still burned, not a whit shorter, and the mass priests muttered; for this had been nothing but an instant as the world measures. I carried the image of the temple down the nave, in my eye. Do you know, my children? The spiritual is to the material, three times real! It was only when I was halfway to my house that I understood the true nature of the vision. As I turned to look once more, and bless, I saw there was something missing. The church was there; but the ultimate prayer, spiring upward from the centre — physically speaking, did not exist at all. And from that moment I knew why God had brought me here, his unworthy servant —" '

The scratchy voice ceased. He heard Father Adam flicking over the unused pages. Then there was silence. He shut his eyes and laid a hand wearily on his forehead.

'I spoke like that once. When I threw myself down and offered myself to the work, I thought that to offer myself was the same as to offer everything. It was my stupidity.'

Father Adam spoke. There was a new note in his voice, astonishment and perturbation.

'But was this all?'

'I thought I was chosen; a spiritual man, loving above all; and given specific work to do.'

'And from this, the rest followed, the debts, the deserted church, discord?'

'More, much more. More than you can ever know. Because I don't really know myself. Reservations, connivances. The work before everything. And woven through it, a golden thread — No. Growth of a plant with strange flowers and fruit, complex, twining, engulfing, destroying, strangling.'

And immediately the plant was visible to him, a riot of foliage and flowers and overripe, bursting fruit. There was no tracing its complications back to the root, no disentangling the anguished faces that cried out from among it; so he cried out himself, and then was silent. He lay, cautious of his back, and avoiding the ache that had started in his forehead, looking only at the stone rib of the vaulting. His one thought was a peculiar one.

I am here; and here is nowhere in particular.

When Father Adam spoke again, his words were no longer scratched. They dropped rather, like little stones.

'So this was all.'

More light came from the window, as Father Adam moved away from it. Now he was close and his next question made no sense.

'When you hear things, do you see them?'

He lay in his nowhere, turning his headache from side to side as though he could shake it off. Footsteps walked past the window, and the looped line of cheerful whistling. Drearily in his head, he watched the whistling disappear round a corner.

'What does it matter?'

'They taught you nothing? All those years ago?'

What did I learn? The eagle stooped on me by the sea. It was enough. And after that —

'You heard her. You know how it was.'

Father Adam whispered passionately.

'It were better a millstone were tied about their necks —'

Oh no, he thought. That's too simple, like every other explanation. That gets nowhere near the root.

But Father Adam was speaking now in open astonishment.

'They never taught you to pray!'

Hair blown back by the wind of the spirit. Mouth open, not for uttering rainwater, but for hosannahs. He smiled wryly at his chaplain.

'It's late days now.'

But Father Adam was not smiling. He was standing sideways, his hands clenched by his chest. He was looking sideways and down out of sufficient face under the wispy hair. This time there was terror in his voice as if he had glimpsed the plant and felt the swift touch of a tendril on his cheek.

'Your confessor —'

'Anselm?'

Always Anselm, he thought. In it, yet not in it; and there is the seal. He spoke to the rib of the vaulting.

'Shall I tell you something, Father Adam? I suspect much and I loved them all; which is perhaps why she haunts me. You are immeasurably better than they are — indeed there may be no people so black, so damned — yet you are not with me, close, caught in the branches. Witchcraft. It must be witchcraft; otherwise how could she and he come so flatly between me and heaven?'

But then he heard breathing close to him. He refocused his eyes from the rib and the past, and saw that Father Adam was kneeling by the bed. His face was covered by his hands and his whole body was shaking. The words were shaken too as they jerked out between the hands, in a sudden mutter.

'God have mercy on us all!'

He took his hands down quickly and crossed himself. He clasped his hands on the bed, bowed his head and muttered again. The muttering slowed, stopped.

Father Adam raised his head. He smiled. Jocelin saw at once how mistaken they were who thought of him as faceless. It was just that what was written there, had been written small in a delicate calligraphy that might easily be overlooked unless one engaged oneself to it deliberately, or looked perforce, as a sick man must look from his bed.

He cried out to the face before he knew he was going to.

'Help me!'

It was as if these words were a key. He felt them shake him as Father Adam had been shaken. The shaking hurt his back and his head; but it was connected to an infinite sea of grief which sent out an arm to fill him and overflowed liberally at his eyes. He let them flow and ignored them for the sea engaged him fully. Then there was another arm; but this one was across his chest, the hand grasping his shoulder. Another hand was wiping his face gently.

After a while the shaking stopped and the water ceased to flow. A voice, delicate as the face, began to murmur by him.

'Now we shall start at the beginning. Once you knew about prayer in all its stages; but you have forgotten. That's good. Most of them are not for ordinary, sinful men. It was a kind of virtue in you. At the lowest level is vocal prayer. It is where we shall start because we are both children, and that is where children start — '

'And *my* prayer, Father? My — vision?'

Then there was a pause. My dark angel will come back, he thought. I know it, I feel the signs in me! Hurry while there's time!

'*My* prayer? My spire of prayer? What you read?'

There was a different wetness, starting this time out of his skin. He felt a hand smoothing the hair from his forehead; but the terror of the angel's approach was on him.

'Quickly!'

'Just above vocal prayer is another stage, very low, and therefore very close. It is where we are given an encouragement, a feeling, an emotion. Just so, you might give a child a spoonful of honey for being good; or just because you loved it. Your prayer was a good prayer certainly; but not very.'

He was turning on the pallet, trying to escape. Only something so deep, it must lie close to the root of the

197

plant, made him cry out to the stone rib and the delicate anxious face.

'My spire pierced every stage, from the bottom to the top!'

Then the dark angel struck him.

CHAPTER ELEVEN

The pain left him sometimes so that he could think. Always his first words were a question to Father Adam.

'Has it fallen yet?'

And the answer was always the same.

'Not yet, my son.'

He was building in his head, examining what foundations should be laid before he could know what he wanted.

'I shall never know the truth until they take the cathedral apart stone by stone like a puzzle.'

But Father Adam must have thought he wandered, for he said nothing. So Jocelin, going his own interior road, came to a second thought.

'And not even then.'

One day he sent for Anselm and waited endlessly under the shadowy vaulting, until he remembered what his new rank was. So he sent again, begging Anselm in charity. So Anselm came stiffly. It was afternoon, and the place already in deep shadow because it faced the east and the cathedral through one window. He heard Father Adam going away down the stairs to leave them together, heard the chair creak as Anselm sank in it. Then he looked towards him, and examined the noble head with its silver fringe of hair above the empty forehead. But Anselm would not look back. He watched the window steadfastly and said nothing.

'Anselm. I've come to a desolate place at last.'

Anselm glanced sideways quickly, then withdrew his eyes as if the sight were improper. His words were what might be expected; but they were dry, stiff as his posture.

'All men at some time or other —'

No, thought Jocelin. That's not how we speak to real men. He doesn't see me. I'm not real; but I'm learning.

'I've been back, so painfully, right back to those days by the sea when you had charge of me.'

Anselm looked his way. There was a kind of stony embarrassment about him; and the words went with them.

'In the midst of life —'

'Life!'

He shut his eyes and thought about it.

'I know of course. My life has been nothing like I thought. But I did walk on the headland once; and I came to you, master of the novices, because I thought the Holy Spirit had chosen us.'

He looked up at the vaulting again. There were stretches of sand and a blinding sea beyond it.

'I ran to you.'

Anselm stirred. There was a slight smile on his face; but it was not a smile of humour.

'You were all over my knees like a dog.'

'What can you see, then, Anselm?'

Anselm was looking out of the window again. There was colour on his cheeks. His voice was stifled.

'Why must you always have a very best friend, like an ignorant girl?'

'I?'

'Why was I the object of this — adolescent regard?'

There was a confusion in Jocelin's head.

'I? Like that?'

Anselm's voice was very low, very bitter.

'You don't know. You've never known how impossible you are. Impossible.'

Jocelin licked his dry lips.

'I am — I was — a man of strong affections. Clumsy.'

He waited for the grief of this to subside a little, then spoke to the vaulting.

'You Anselm. On your side.'

Anselm stood up and began to pace round the room. At last he stopped, between Jocelin's face and the vaulting. He turned his stiff neck, looked Jocelin in the eye, then flinched away again.

'It's so long ago. Perhaps it never meant much — and then, all the things that came after! No. I can't say more. Amused and touched. And irritated. You were so — keen.'

'Keen. Just keen. Nothing more. You saw nothing, you understood nothing.'

Anselm cried out.

'And can't *you* understand? You sat on our necks, on my neck, for a generation!'

'There was our work to be done. I thought so — and now I don't know what I think —'

'That place was well enough for me; though perhaps not precisely what the founder intended. Then you had to come, flying like a great bird —'

'— to the master of the novices.'

'I am what I am But to see you skipping up through purely nominal steps, acolyte, deacon, priest; to see you dean of this church when you could hardly read Our Father; and to be tempted, yes tempted — for where the horse goes, the wagon must follow — and one must admit that the great world is necessary since we're none of us saints — tempted towards a sort of ruin. I admit it freely. I might have remained where I was and done some good. You tempted me and I did eat.'

'Then?'

'Then? Why you know the rest. The old king died; and you rose no further.'

'I see.'

'And after that, to have to hear your confessions, your partial, self-congratulatory confessions —'

Even in his weakness a vast astonishment fell on Jocelin.

'What kind of a priest are you?'

'You should know. The same sort as you, if you like. Minimal. I know it. What about Ivo, Jocelin? A boy canon. Just because his father gave timber for the building. You see? He's got as much right in the church as you had. Or I have. Only he'll do less harm. He spends his time hunting. You've lain on us like a blight. There have been times when the sight of you in your authority has squeezed this heart of mine small and made my breath come short. I'll tell you another thing. For all that stone contraption which hangs out there over our deliberations, there's a peace and amity in Chapter because you're not there, as if balm had been spilt.'

'Anselm!'

'Do you remember what you said in Chapter when I spoke against the spire? Because I do. I shall never forget. There, before all of them. "Sit down, Anselm!" Do you remember that? *"Sit down, Anselm —"* '

'Let's leave it at that. There's nothing to be said or done.'

'And there's the matter of the candles.'

'I know.'

'And finally, Jocelin, if you want every matter out in the open, there's the business of the building.'

'Can't you go?'

'You must admit it capped everything, to try and make a man of my years and standing into a builder's mate.'

'Well. Forgive me, then.'

'Naturally I forgive you. I forgive you.'

'I beg you. No forgiveness for this or that, for this candle or that insult. Forgive me for being what I am.'

'I said so.'

'Do you feel it Anselm? Tell me you feel it!'

There were steps going down the stair; and after that, a long silence.

It was many minutes before he felt a change; but then people came and danced before his eyes, a strange ducking and weaving. Among them he could see no one clearly but Father Adam; and he cried out again.

'Help me, Father!'

Then Father Adam came close and began to unravel things. He pulled and unravelled but got nowhere because all things were so mixed and the evil plant grew among and over them all. So in the end Jocelin felt nothing but the pain of his back (and the sick fire when they turned him over to pack it with lamb's wool) and apart from that, a dissolved grief from throat to navel. Father Adam could see nothing on his hands; but told him he was weak and deluded and that all that mattered was the will. Nor did Father Adam understand how necessary it was to have forgiveness from those who were not christian souls; nor how for that it was necessary to understand them; nor how impossible understanding them was.

At this point Jocelin grew very cunning, for he saw that he would have to escape from Father Adam. He waited for a good day; for there were occasional good days, when the sun lay glossily on the floor and he knew exactly where he was. When one came, he pretended to sleep an exhausted sleep while he heard Father Adam rustling. He opened one eye secretly and watched the little man's back as it went away down the stairs. He mustered his strength for the endeavour, and at last he got up, slewing his legs off the bed, and waiting for his faintness to go away. He felt along by the wall, placed his skullcap among his hair, and hung his cloak on his shoulders. He crawled down the stairs, with the hinges of his legs trembling for weakness, and the great hall was empty. There was no fire and no candles; but there was much light and shadows moving over the windows. Also there was a freshness about the air that stirred the grief in his chest. He got a stick from the mass on the hearth and pressed himself up by it.

He waited for a while, thinking. I will go out by the back way so that he won't see me; and I shan't have to see the stone hammer.

Outside the door there was a woodstack among long, rank grass. A scent struck him, so that he leaned against the woodstack, careless of his back, and waited while the dissolved grief welled out of his eyes. Then there was a movement over his head so that for an instant he had a wild hope. He twisted his neck and looked up sideways. There was a cloud of angels flashing in the sunlight, they were pink and gold and white; and they were uttering this sweet scent for joy of the light and the air. They brought with them a scatter of clear leaves, and among the leaves a long, black springing thing. His head swam with the angels, and suddenly he understood there was

204

more to the appletree than one branch. It was there beyond the wall, bursting up with cloud and scatter, laying hold of the earth and the air, a fountain, a marvel, an appletree; and this made him weep in a childish way so that he could not tell whether he was glad or sorry. Then, where the yard of the deanery came to the river and trees lay over the sliding water, he saw all the blue of the sky condensed to a winged sapphire, that flashed once.

He cried out.

'Come back!'

But the bird was gone, an arrow shot once. It will never come back, he thought, not if I sat here all day. He began to play with the thought that the bird might return, to sit on a post only a few yards away in all its splendour, but his heart knew better.

'No kingfisher will return for me.'

All the same, he said to himself, I was lucky to see it. No one else saw it. At last he got to his feet and went out by the sideway to the close. He watched the dusty end of his stick and his feet moving slowly. I must look like an old crow, he thought, inching along and bent nearly double. Why do I go to find something that isn't there? And even that's too simple! I go for many reasons and they're all mixed up. Father Adam was right. I make too much fuss among the appletrees and the kingfishers.

When he came to the King's Gate he rested on a convenient mounting block and examined the dust. But for all the feet that had trodden it, it remained ordinary dust, which seemed to make everything much sadder. So he braced himself and shuffled through the dust until there was the running gutter of the high street under his nose, with a naked child playing in it.

He spoke to her.

'Where is Roger Mason, my child?'

Well now, he thought, who would have believed I could sound so much like an old man? But while he was thinking this, the child splashed out of the gutter and ran away. Then, since he had no other means of crossing, he walked through the gutter. He found the legs and waist of a man and spoke to him.

'Where is Roger Mason, my son?'

Someone spat from above him so that the spittle hung on the edge of his cloak. A voice spoke gruffly.

'New Street.'

The legs went away.

He turned his stick and his feet to the right and made them move over the cobbles. New Street is very long, he thought; and when he thought that, it appeared to him that he could go no further. He peered round him for a mounting block but found none. Then he sank down by a wall of wattle and daub with his cloak covering him. He drew it across his face so that he was in a tent.

But he felt the pressure of their presence even through the tent; and presently he looked out, to see the naked feet of children.

'Where is Roger Mason, my children?'

The feet went away, splashing in the gutter. A stone bounced by his feet. I had best go, he thought — go somewhere. So he laboured up by the wall; and immediately he remembered that Roger Mason would be in Letoyle. He crept along, his stick out to the left and a hand out to the wall on the right; and at last he saw the inn with the painted star on the sign and a mounting block outside. He sat breathlessly on the stone, saying to himself; It is just as well since I can go no further.

'Roger Mason.'

Feet went away and returned with more feet and he spoke to them, as before.

'Roger Mason. Roger Mason.'

At last there were woman's feet among the rest, and the hem of a red dress. The woman cried out and talked busily; but her words were easy to ignore as always. I am sorry for her, he thought, but not much — just a little sorry. It is my deficiency that she has no part in my grief.

Hands took him under the armpits and lifted him away from the block with his feet and his stick dragging. He saw a door approach, and stairs on which his feet touched one by one, while his stick went tap, bounce, tap. Then there was another door in comparative darkness, which swung open. Hands lowered him in a cloud of faintness to a settle, then went away and shut the door. He waited with his eyes shut for things to come back to him.

The first thing that came back was a noise. It was a scraping, a tussing, a thing of breath and phlegm, and rhythmical. It opened his eyes for him; and there, on one side of the small fire, opposite to the window, was a great bed of crumpled linen with a bolster. Roger Mason lay in it on one elbow, fully dressed except for his boots. He was laughing endlessly out of his swollen face; and then his mouth was wider open, the laugh more like a shout, and he fell back, prone. Jocelin watched his chest moving up and down.

Roger Mason rolled over, turning the bedclothes with him. He got heavily on one elbow again and grinned at Jocelin like a dog. There was sweat on his face. As Jocelin looked into the redrimmed eyes, he saw the face twist. Roger Mason turned his head sideways and spat inaccurately at the fire.

'You stink like a corpse.'

Jocelin examined the words and then a memory of the faces over his bed. It may be so, he thought, yes indeed, it may be so. He heard his voice echo the words in a foolish, old man's voice.

'It may be so Roger, it may be so. Yes indeed, it may be so.'

Roger Mason leaned forward over his elbow. He sounded deeply satisfied.

'They got you too.'

He belched, and a red liquid ran down his chin.

'It hasn't fallen yet Roger. Father Adam told me so. He said it would fall some day even if we'd built it of adamant and anchored it to the roots of the earth.'

The master builder began to heave on the bed. He wrenched his feet away from the clothes and staggered across the room. Jocelin heard him cursing and banging at the window. There came a crash, then the tinkle of glass. The master builder mouthed at the unechoing air.

'Fall when you like, me old cock!'

'There's very little wind today, Roger. Enough to make the apple blossom dance.'

The master builder came lurching back. He fell heavily on his knees by the bed, and pawed at it. He gave up, slumped sideways, and laughed again.

'I like your stink, Jocelin. It does me good. I didn't think there was much could do me good.'

But Jocelin was away in some dream, out of which he answered absently.

'I saw a kingfisher.'

Then there were more feet, a red dress, talk, talk, talk. Roger Mason was being helped on to the bed again. The voice came and talked at Jocelin, left him and went back to the bed.

'Don't you understand, you great fool? They know he's here!'

Then the dress and the voice went away through the door. He looked across at the bed but could see little but a chest that went up and down, could hear nothing but gasp, pause, gasp.

'Roger? Roger? Can you hear me?'

Nothing but gasp.

'Imagine it. I thought I was doing a great work; and all I was doing was bringing ruin and breeding hate. Roger?'

He watched closely, but the only movement he could see other than the up and down of the chest was a slight quivering of one hand at each gasp. He turned his eyes away and watched the embers of the fire instead. They seemed brighter now, because shadows were creeping into every corner.

'To love all men with a holy love. And then — Roger, can you hear me?'

But Roger never stirred. Jocelin gave up the attempt and waited, while the hand lay among the gasps, the fire brightened among shadows, and he examined the formless and inexpressible mass that lay in his mind.

At last the figure on the bed stirred. Roger Mason lay slack, his head on the bolster, his face looking at Jocelin expressionlessly.

'Well. Here we are, the two of us.'

'It's not true the old don't suffer. They suffer as much as the young and they've less capacity to deal with it.'

'Big talk.'

'And then, after all the bogus sanctity, to be bewitched by a dead woman.'

'You're mad. I always said so.'

'Perhaps. All the time I was busy with that colossal

209

spike — Yet I knew nothing of her. Is that what she meant, in my, my dream, speaking to me, or rather not speaking, but humming at me from her empty mouth? And yet you see, I'm not sure of that even. Alison said she bewitched me. That's what it was, wasn't it, Roger? What else could it be? And yet you see — it may be a true Nail after all. There's just no way of knowing.'

The master builder shouted.

'God damn you Jocelin! It'll fall, and I'll have to wait for it! You took my craft, you took my army, you took everything. May you be cursed right through hell!'

He gave a hiccuping sob.

'You and your net. You drove me too high.'

'I was driven too. I was in some net or other.'

He heard Roger sniffing into the bolster.

'Too high. Too high.'

All at once there was a clearness in Jocelin's head. He saw exactly what could be done with one bulk of the formless, the incommunicable.

'Look. This is one thing I came to do.'

He picked at the morse until his cloak fell from him, pushed off his skullcap, and laid the cross from his chest on the settle.

'I'm sorry about the tonsure. Clean water through the mouth of a dead dog. No, indeed. Heresies? I'm a compendium.'

He got up and shuffled across the room. He knelt, but there was not enough strength in his back to sustain his weight so he fell on his hands. Well, he thought, this will have to do.

'Once you said I was the devil himself. It isn't true. I'm a fool. Also I think — I'm a building with a vast cellarage where the rats live; and there's some kind of blight on my hands. I injure everyone I touch, particularly those I love. Now I've come in pain and shame, to ask you to forgive me.'

There was a long silence. The fire clicked, the window creaked on its hinges, and the leaves stirred outside. He examined the floorboards between his hands. I'm here, he thought. I can do no more.

There was a thump from the floor as a knee hit it by his right hand. His shoulders were seized and he was hauled up straight. Roger's arms were round him, in the flames of his back. He felt his body and head shaken as the master builder cursed and sobbed. He did not sob well, so that each sob was a convulsion that shook them both; and then words came tumbling out between the sobs so that Jocelin found he was clinging too, with a drowning clutch. Roger's head was ground into his shoulder and he found himself babbling foolish things about an appletree, saying foolish, nursery things and patting a broad, shaking back. He is such a good man, he thought, so good — whatever that is! Something is being born here under the painted, swinging sign.

Presently Roger heaved himself back. He kept one hand on Jocelin's shoulder, but smeared the other over his own face.

'Blubbering like a baby. It's the drink. I cry easily when I'm drunk.'

Jocelin found himself swaying under the heavy hand.

'D'you think you could help me up, Roger?'

The master builder gave a great shout of laughter. He half-carried Jocelin back to the settle, then went and slumped on the edge of the bed. All the time, Jocelin explained.

'There isn't much to my back nowadays. You could snap me. Sometimes I think it's the weight of the stone hammer; but there it is.'

'There it is. Sticking up. Drink.'

'Not for me. No thank you.'

A stray end of a faggot caught and burned with a yellow flame. It filled the room with leaping shadows. The master builder reached for the jug and took a swig at it.

'We did what we could.'

'Things were terrible right at the top. Insane.'

'Don't talk about it.'

'Heavy; pause. Light; pause.'

The master builder shouted.

'All right! All right!'

Jocelin inspected the formless thing in his head again.

'There's more of course. It'll fall one day; but for all the bending pillars, the slanting spire, the rubble — I don't know. I've still a residue of, what shall I call it, disbelief perhaps? You see it *may* be what we were meant to do, the two of us. He said I'm like a girl, I always have to have a best friend; but there's nothing wrong in that, is there? So I gave it my body. What holds it up, Roger? I? The nail? Does she, or do you? Or is it poor Pangall, crouched beneath the crossways, with a sliver of mistletoe between his ribs?'

Roger Mason went very still, so still the flames made him shake as if he were part of the wall. But there were other things moving in the room, Jocelin felt them beating about him with black wings. His voice spoke out of a storm and he hardly knew he was using it.

'So there's still something you can do, Roger my son. Still something.'

Roger Mason's face was dark again with blood, and his voice hoarse.

'That was what you came for, wasn't it, Jocelin? An eye for an eye, tooth for tooth. If I don't — you'll tell.'

212

'No! No! I never meant —'

'I understand you, Father. I've felt it catching up.'

Now, among the black wings, terror fell on Jocelin.

'I didn't mean —'

'I said I understand you.'

'Something made me say it — something out of my control!'

Roger Mason had slumped on the bed.

'When the next gale begins, I shall remember. An eye for an eye.'

'You could go away. You're still young.'

'Who'd employ me? Who'd work with me? You want everything, don't you, Father?'

'God is all about us. That I *knew* — But I know these other things as well. Which is to say, I know nothing. What's a man's mind Roger? Is it the whole building, cellarage and all?'

Then the woman was in the room, darkeyed and speaking windily. When she had gone he heard other voices and laughter.

'What's that outside?'

'People.'

'You see — if she knew anything about it; what can I say? The trouble is, Roger, that the cellarage knew about him — knew he was impotent I mean — and arranged the marriage. It was her hair, I think. I used to see it, blowing red about a thin, pale face. After that, of course not. But later when she stood by the pillar looking across at you, it seared into my eye. Then she bewitched me. She must have done, mustn't she? That's why I must know what kind of creature she was; because if she knew, knew what happened to her husband, even consented to it perhaps — there would be no horror as deep — And of course a creature like that would haunt me!'

'What are you talking about?'

'About her, of course. I got to look for her. She'd come running and then stand. I bound up her cut knee with a piece torn from my own — Well, what of it? Later, when I knew how deeply she was in my net, I tried to see her, tried to explain —'

'*You?*'

'Did she ever speak of me? Well never mind. I sacrificed her too. Deliberately. You know Roger, prayers are answered. That's horrible. So after she died, she haunted me, she bewitched me. To have prayer blinded by hair. A dead woman. That's a good joke, isn't it?'

'A joke!'

'There ought to be some mode of life where all love is good, where one love can't compete with another but adds to it. What kind of a thing is a man's mind, Roger?'

'You got what you came for. Go, now.'

'Only I must know —'

'What does it matter to us now?'

'There's so much confusion in my mind. I loved her, you see, before she bewitched me, like a daughter. You see, that time she died —'

'Let it be. Go.'

'I need three tongues to say three things at once. I was there. You remember? I only wanted to help. Perhaps I understood some things, even then. She was on the floor. When she looked up, she saw me in the doorway, all dressed up, dean, priest, the accuser. I only wanted to help, but it killed her. I killed her as surely as if I'd cut her throat.'

He heard the master builder's feet by his own. He felt a hot and winy breath by his face.

'Get out.'

'Can't you see? It's why I must know these things — I killed her!'

Suddenly the master builder was shouting.

'Get out! Get out!'

His hands hurled Jocelin sideways. The door slammed open and the same hands thrust him away. He saw stairs coming at him far too fast; then he was clinging to a rail, and his knees were on the stairs.

'You stinking corpse!'

The jug flew past his head and shattered on the wall. His feet and hands took him down to greasy cobbles and he heard the master builder shouting behind him.

'I hope they flay you!'

But that noise was consumed in a storm of voices, all shouting and laughing and making hound noises. He got up by the wall, but the noises swirling round him, brought hands and feet and dim faces at his own. He glimpsed a dark alley and pushed himself at it while the clothing tore cn his back. He heard his gown rip; he could not lie down for hands held him up. The noises began to bray and yelp. They created their own mouths, fanged and slavering. He cried out.

'My children! My children!'

The yelling and bundling went on, a sea of imprecation and hate. The hands became fists and feet. High over everything he thought he heard Ivo and his friends urging on the hounds.

'Loo! Loo! Loo!'

He was flat on his face, he was looking at legs and the light from a doorway on the filth of the gutter.

Then there was a spreading silence. The legs moved away from him, little by little. He heard a voice in the silence, a woman's voice.

'Holy Mother of God. Look at his back!'

215

The feet moved more quickly. They went out of his eyes, and he heard them going, running, rushing, stumbling over the cobbles. The lighted door slammed shut.

He lay there for a while, shivering. At last he began to move, crawling towards the wall. I am naked, he thought, that was to be expected. He pulled himself up and began to edge towards the faint lights from the cressets in the High Street. At times he fell away from the wall, staggered into the gutter and out again; though once he fell in it. Here I show what I am, he thought, and climbed out again. At the place where the alley met the High Street, he fell and did not move. He was hardly conscious of the cloth placed over his back, and of the hem of Rachel's skirt and the sandalled feet of Father Adam. Hands began to care for him gently. A voice began to babble like the gutter in winter. Then he was swamped by clouds of darkness.

CHAPTER TWELVE

H e was facing the stone rib of the vaulting again. It had changed in no way but he himself had entered some new kind of life. This was a sense of suspension above the body, which every now and then would be engulfed by an irresistible wave of faintness which brought a mindless fear with it. After the faintness, there would be a gap. Then he would find himself suspended in consciousness again, and wondering vaguely what had happened. He would speak wordlessly to himself above the body.

Where was I then?

And always, the answer would come, wordlessly.

Nowhere.

There was a bitter stuff to drink, poppy perhaps, which he thought sometimes, was what allowed him to drift and swim so above the prone body. There were faces that interposed themselves too, one which gave him the drink, and another, Father Adam, now fully in focus. He could not tell how wide the gaps were, nor how long the periods of suspension and drifting. Only he would note, without surprise between one glance and the next, how the sunlight or shadow had measured off hours on the ribs of the vaulting. Sometimes he would be more immediately aware of the thing, the mechanism that lay beneath him. It was concerned above all with the business of stretching and collapsing the ribs, a task which it did ceaselessly but feebly and the heart at the centre fluttered like a bird caught in a window. But he was fetched down into his body only when the ministers laid hands on him for some necessary office. Once he heard a conversation clearly and understood only the last few words.

'It is a wasting, a consumption of the back and spine —'

Then after a pause : 'No. None whatever. His heart, you see.'

But most of the curious, fluctuating time, he was suspended above his body or in the gap. He had thoughts that lasted a century or a second. He saw images to which now he was wholly indifferent. He said almost nothing, because speech was so complex, even when you only had access to one mouth. His access was limited by a desire to avoid the trap of the body down there — limited also by the gap that so often ambushed him. Nevertheless, every few centuries among the mists and the matter-of-fact examinations of the vaulting, he would make the long effort. He would pull himself down into the stone mouth, would break up the stone, and eject a puff of shaped air.

'Fallen?'

The focused face of Father Adam would come close, leaning down, smiling.

'Not yet.'

He would examine the blue eyes, the mouth stretched ever so slightly by the smile into the pucker of the cheeks. Then when the face had slid sideways out of sight, he would find himself examining whatever had come to take its place — a stone rib, with perhaps a fly landing upside down and occupying itself with some small business.

At one point he began to think about his tomb and managed to send for the dumb man. Through an interminable succession of time and gap he got him to understand what was wanted; himself without ornament, lying stripped in death of clothing and flesh, a prone skeleton lapped in skin, head fallen back, mouth open. He plucked at the bedclothes, and at last hands understood. They stripped him for the young man, who drew with a face of fascinated disgust while Jocelin drifted away again. After a century or two the young man had gone, and a fly cleaned its legs on the vaulting.

Once there were candles, voices murmuring, and the touch of oil. He floated above the unction which had relevance to nothing but the leaden body; and a gap came. But when he woke and floated again there was a new thing. He could hear wind and rain, and the window drumming. Then he remembered the cellarage and the rats in it and the panic of that flung him right back into the gasping body.

'Mason. Roger Mason.'

Faces came close to his, enquiring with raised eyebrows, and speaking long, incomprehensible sentences.

'Roger Mason!'

All at once the gasping caught up with the words and the thoughts in his head. His chest declined its work so that he drove it in fear. He felt hands lift him up so that he was sitting.

Then he was lying on his back again, looking up at a stone rib where the glossy sunlight was shifting line by line.

Where was I then?

But a face came between him and the sunlight, leaning down, shaken, redrimmed as to the eyes, the black hair fallen in snakes that brushed over him, the mouth flashing open and shut. There was a wildness about her attack that made him indifferent to it, since he could not follow it successively.

'In the outhouse between the onions and a sack of wheat —'

How will she ever be rid of so much life? She is a devouring mouth, a good woman.

'— on his hands and knees. The rope was still round his neck and a broken rafter on the other end of it. He always said the most difficult thing in his business was to estimate a breaking strain, though God knows —'

God, thought Jocelin, as his mind saw things small, God? If I could go back, I would take God as lying between people and to be found there. But now witchcraft hides Him.

'Sits by the fire, his head on one side, blind and dumb — I have to do everything for him, everything! Do you understand? Like a baby!'

He noted without interest how the hands of Father Adam pulled her sideways from him, heard her high sobbing in the room, then diminishing down the stairs. He saw in some mode, the face of Roger Mason beyond communication, the children on the grass, the body of Pangall crouched in its vigil. He saw the clumsy platforms of the tower, the ungainly and splintered octagons. He felt the weight.

No more, he thought, no more. I can't even feel for them. Or for myself.

Someone was muttering in the room and there was the clink of metal. The face of Father Adam came close again. He watched the lips and they let out a sound, but he was too weary to pay attention to it.

The blue eyes blinked once. Wrinkles appeared in the skin outside them. The lips opened and shut again. This time his poppied ears caught the word before it vanished into the vaulting.

'Jocelin.'

Then he knew that the great revolution of his clock was accomplished; and dying seemed easy as eating or drinking or easing, one thing to be taken after another.

Only the present knowledge was a kind of freedom so that his thoughts went trotting away like a horse unharnessed from the cart. He looked up experimentally to see if at this late hour the witchcraft had left him; and there was a tangle of hair, blazing among the stars; and the great club of his spire lifted towards it. That's all, he thought, that's the explanation if I had time: and he made a word for Father Adam.

'Berenice.'

The smile became puzzled and anxious. Then it cleared.

'Saint?'

Out of all the complex of weaknesses and defences, the labouring body contracted the chest, trying to laugh; and he stilled it in sudden fear, balancing himself in life like a juggler; and he had a sudden liking for Father Adam and desired to give him something; so when he was properly balanced, he made another word for him.

'Saint.'

And dying is more natural than living, because what could be more unnatural than that panicstricken thing leaping and falling like a last flame beneath the ribs?

'Jocelin.'

That is my name, he thought, and he looked at Father Adam with mild interest; since Father Adam was dying too; and tomorrow or some such time a voice would say 'Adam' in the same tone as to a child. No matter how high he rises, robe after robe, tomorrow or the day after they will tap three times on the smooth parchment of

that forehead with the silver hammer. Then his mind
trotted away again and he saw what an extraordinary
creature Father Adam was, covered in parchment from
head to foot, parchment stretched or tucked in, with
curious hairs on top and a mad structure of bones to keep
it apart. Immediately, as in a dream that came between
him and the face, he saw all people naked, creatures of
light brown parchment, which bound in their pipes or
struts. He saw them pace or prance in sheets of woven
stuff, with the skins of dead animals under their feet and
he began to struggle and gasp to leave this vision behind
him in words that never reached the air.

*How proud their hope of hell is. There is no innocent work.
God knows where God may be.*

Arms wrestled him down, and there was a gap. But he
came back in a panic, to see it through.

'Now Jocelin, we are going to help you into heaven.'

Heaven, thought Jocelin busily in the panic, you who
bind me, you who won't die until tomorrow, what do you
know about heaven? Heaven and hell and purgatory are
small and bright as a jewel in someone's pocket only to
be taken out and worn on feast days. This is a grey, suc-
cessive day for dying on. And what is heaven to me unless
I go in holding him by one hand and her by the other?

Assent?

I traded a stone hammer for four people.

Suddenly he found he had to bite the air, bite and hold
on. Hands were heaving him upright so that his chest
got air for a moment without his trying. The panic went
out of his chest but beat about him.

There were two eyes looking at him through the
panic. They were the only steady things, and before
them, he was like a building about to fall. They looked
in, an eye for an eye, one eye for each eye. He bit more

222

air and clung to the eyes with his own as the only steady things in living.

The two eyes slid together.

It was the window, bright and open. Something divided it. Round the division was the blue of the sky. The division was still and silent, but rushing upward to some point at the sky's end, and with a silent cry. It was slim as a girl, translucent. It had grown from some seed of rosecoloured substance that glittered like a waterfall, an upward waterfall. The substance was one thing, that broke all the way to infinity in cascades of exultation that nothing could trammel.

The panic beat and swept in, struck the window into patches that danced before either eye; but not the panic nor the blindness could diminish the terror of it and the astonishment

'Now — I know nothing at all.'

But arms were laying down a whirl of terror and astonishment, down, down. Wild flashes of thought split the darkness. Our very stones cry out.

'I believe, Jocelin, I believe!'

What is terror and joy, how should they be mixed, why are they the same, the flashing, the flying through the panicshot darkness like a bluebird over water?

'A gesture of assent —'

In the tide, flying like a bluebird, struggling, shouting, screaming to leave behind the words of magic and incomprehension —

It's like the appletree!

Father Adam, leaning down, could hear nothing. But he saw a tremor of the lips that might be interpreted as a cry of: *God! God! God!* So of the charity to which he had access, he laid the Host on the dead man's tongue.